# TO BECOME A BROTHER

LINDY BELL

sDay Agency Publishing
Salt Lake City, UT
84065

Editor: Sean Linton

Cover Design:
Dar Albert, Wicked Smart Designs, www.wickedsmartdesigns.com
Paperback and Digital Formatting:
Dayna Linton, Day Agency, www.dayagency.com

Library of Congress Control Number: Pending

ISBN: 978-1-7365604-6-4 (Paperback)
ISBN: 978-1-7365604-7-1 (Digital Book)

First Edition: 2024

10 9 8 7 6 5 4 3 2 1
Printed in the USA

*For my Great Nephew Bennett Bell
and Great Niece Emma Bell*

*You have impressed and encouraged me not only with your enthusiastic support for my first young adult book but with your insightful and timely suggestions that helped me bring Lucas more vividly to life through your eyes. It began with the first draft and continued through answering my many questions, giving your thoughts, and sharing your ideas. You inspired me and helped me every step of the way. Thank you, Bennett and Emma— I love you and am so incredibly proud of the young man and woman you are!!*

# AUTHOR'S NOTE

*To Become A Brother* is a work of fiction. Any resemblance to actual events or persons is entirely coincidental. As a note, Fentanyl is a potent and dangerous drug. Its use in any form is strongly discouraged without proper supervision by a medical professional. Foster parents hold the precious bud of a life in their hands. That child may not be theirs biologically but they are theirs to nurture and train up in the way they should go. It's an awesome and weighty responsibility. Thank you, foster parents, for loving and nurturing the child (or children) in your care.

# TO BECOME A BROTHER

TEARS PRICKED LUCAS' EYES as he stared blindly out the bus window into the bleak winter sky. The smell of diesel mixed with the garlic and onion drifting off the old man in the seat in front of him. Lucas never cried. He wouldn't allow himself to cry. He just couldn't. His mom, sitting in the seat next to him, patted him gently on his knee. He looked up and did his best to smile, but she just looked away. Lucas' smile disappeared too, turning back to look out the window.

His mom used to be happy. She'd always laughed and teased him and his dad. But that seemed like a long time ago. The happiness and laughter ended the day his dad was killed in a training accident at the Army base where they'd lived. Lucas wasn't sure what happened. His mom just said his dad wouldn't be coming home again. After that, she turned into someone Lucas barely recognized. She didn't smile or laugh any more. She seemed to just . . . *exist* without really being aware of what went on around her. Lucas soon realized he would need to take care of *her* now.

Lucas hadn't been happy since that day either, at least not until he and his mom moved to Abernathy, and he started second grade in Mrs. Garrett's class. Mrs. Garrett reminded him of how his mom used to be—fun, happy, and always with a bright smile. Mrs. Garrett was also nice and pretty and made him feel smart. But mostly, she made him feel noticed and important. Being at school and away from the dreary apartment his mom had rented for them felt almost as if life was a bit normal again. Coming to school was actually fun, and he always looked forward to seeing Mrs. Garrett and getting to eat lunch with Mr. Andy. Mr. Andy was Mrs. Garrett's husband and a real firefighter. They'd decided—together—that Lucas would call him Mr. Andy. Firefighter Garrett seemed like too much to say and Firefighter Andy didn't sound quite right either.

While they ate lunch, Mr. Andy talked with him like they were equals. Lucas felt like he could tell Mr. Andy anything, and Mr. Andy would understand. And he usually did. Lucas wanted to remember everything he could about their talks because what Mr. Andy said always seemed so important; such as how tough things had been for Mr. Andy as he grew up and how similar his situation was to Lucas' situation. Lucas especially wanted to remember Mr.

Andy's words of advice. He had a feeling, just a feeling, that he'd need those words of advice someday.

Lucas smiled thinking of how Mr. Andy made him laugh, but he especially remembered the things Mr. Andy said about being a firefighter. Lucas knew by listening to Mr. Andy and his stories, that he wanted to be *just like* Mr. Andy and be a firefighter too. Mr. Andy had said the biggest and most important thing about being a firefighter was getting to help people, and Lucas knew—that's what he wanted to do too. He wanted to help people.

Lucas sighed and carefully opened the hinged lid of the metal box he clutched tightly in his lap. His treasure box. He pulled out a red construction paper leaf and ran his fingers lightly over Mrs. Garrett's writing that said *Mr. Andy and Fire Trucks*. He carefully placed the leaf back in the box and then pulled out a pencil with a fire hydrant eraser on top. He twirled it slowly between his fingers, thinking about the field trip Mrs. Garrett's class had taken to the fire station. He'd gotten to sit in the seat of a real fire truck and tried on a real bunker coat. It had been heavy and way too big, but he'd loved the feel of it. But the very best thing about the field trip was being with Mr. Andy and standing proudly at his side.

Returning the pencil to the box, Lucas took out a small, wrinkled picture that'd been torn in half. He smiled wistfully—Jill Barkley. They'd met in first grade at the Army base elementary school and up until he and his mom moved, he and Jill had been inseparable. He grinned slightly, remembering when Jill had walked up to him at lunch one day, a sucker in her mouth. "Your hair is too long," she'd stated matter-of-factly by way of introduction.

"Well, your hair is too...too blonde," Lucas had replied weakly.

Jill, with her long blonde hair, blue eyes and beautiful smile, had laughed, a pretty sparkling laugh, and Lucas had laughed too. But now, he just smiled sadly. Even after all these years, he still missed her. Looking down at the picture, he remembered the afternoon it'd been taken. He was at Jill's house, as he was almost every day after school. Jill's mom, Jessica, had just taken a pan of cookies out of the oven when Dan, Jill's dad, came through and snatched one from the pan. He'd started dancing around, tossing the cookie from hand to hand because it was still hot. Lucas remembered all of them laughing and then laughing even harder when they'd all started dancing around the kitchen, mimicking him. That was when Jill's mom had snapped the photo.

Lucas sighed. He couldn't remember the last time he'd laughed like that. After Jill showed the picture to him, she'd torn it in two, giving him the half with her and keeping the one of him for herself. "This way, we'll always be with each other," she'd said, kissing him lightly on the cheek, giggling.

Lucas blinked back his tears. He carefully placed the picture back into the box and snapped the lid shut with a soft click.

The bus door hissed closed and after a minute or two the bus jerked into motion, yanking Lucas reluctantly back to the present. His legs dangled over the edge of the seat while he ran the fingers of one hand aimlessly along its textured gray upholstery. Everything seemed gray including the steely gray of the cloudy sky outside the bus window. He watched the bus terminal and the parking lot roll by as they pulled onto the main road and then onto the highway that would take him further and further from Mrs. Garrett, Mr. Andy, and Abernathy. Lucas clenched his hands into fists on top of his treasure box, the rhythm of the tires humming around him as they started to roll down the highway. He leaned his head against the cold window and squeezed his eyes tight, making a promise to himself. He was going to become a firefighter, just like Mr. Andy, and when he did, he was coming back to Abernathy to surprise Mr. Andy and Mrs. Garrett. He couldn't wait.

L ucas' head popped back sharply with the impact of the boy's fist, as stars sprung before his eyes. He'd been hit there before. It wouldn't have hurt so badly this time if his new foster father hadn't already slapped him in that same spot that morning. Lucas shook his head, his mop of golden-brown hair swinging loosely. He staggered backwards, not realizing the stouter guy he'd already knocked down was already back on his feet. Before Lucas could dodge the blow, the heavier bully punched him viciously in the stomach, sending Lucas to his knees, gulping for air. A third bully took the opportunity to jam his knee into the side of Lucas' face, sending him rolling onto his side. Still trying to catch his breath, Lucas lay in the middle of the dirty alley behind the school, struggling to get to his feet while he cradled his stomach.

"Is that all ya got?" the taller of the three, Joel De Grey, taunted. Lucas hazarded a quick glance up at the one who'd spoken. About Lucas' height, this guy was slender but powerfully athletic. His dark hair had been smoothed back but now hung loosely into his face. From his looks, Lucas thought this guy would probably be someone the girls would like, but right now, he had a distasteful sneer on his face as he loomed over Lucas.

"Come on. You're so full of big talk. Let's see you back it up," the stouter of the three, Marty Pierce said, his cold, steel-gray eyes narrowing in a glare. He shoved Lucas down after Lucas managed to get to one knee. Lucas hit the gritty pavement hard, again, hoping but knowing, they weren't done.

The third bully, Tony Harlow, stood back, rubbing his fist from a punch he'd landed directly to Lucas' jaw. He was the smallest of the three but surprisingly strong. His face and nose were covered with freckles as he grinned tauntingly down at Lucas.

"What's the matter? Trying to be the big hero butting into our business? You're new here. We suggest you keep your nose in your own business. That is . . . if you don't want more of the same," the first guy with the long dark hair said, kicking Lucas once more.

Lucas gasped as he collapsed onto the pavement, pain shooting through him once more.

The three exchanged a quick look before they took off running in the opposite direction from where excited voices could be heard approaching.

Lucas moaned and tried to move, dragging himself painfully to a sitting position. He drew the back of his hand across his bottom lip, pulling it away to see a streak of bright red blood mixed with caked dirt. His worn jeans now had a hole in each knee, and his shirt was torn in a couple of places. His wardrobe was getting smaller. His only other pair of jeans were too short and both of his other shirts were old and faded. He was unlikely to get more clothes any time soon.

The excited voices grew louder until a group of students raced around the corner, heading toward him with the school's police officer in the lead. The officer skidded to a halt and knelt beside Lucas. A brass name plate with 'Jenkins' was pinned to his dark blue uniform. Officer Jenkins was a slender young man with dark brown hair, a strong jaw and hazel eyes that were studying Lucas closely with concern.

Putting a hand on Lucas' shoulder and bending down eye level, he said, "Just stay where you are. The school nurse is on the way. I'm Officer Jenkins. I haven't seen you around before. Are you new here at Baker Heights?"

Lucas nodded, guessing that was the name of the school. There'd been so many over the past few years, he couldn't keep up with the names.

"Can you tell me your name?" Officer Jenkins asked gently as the students crowded closer. He motioned for them to back up. "Let's give him some room, okay? And don't you guys have class in a few minutes? Go. I've got it from here."

"Now," he said with a pointed look.

The students moaned their objection, but Officer Jenkins cocked his head. "Go!"

As the students reluctantly began to disperse, Lucas slowly stood, clasping his torso where the stouter bully had landed his punch, and tried to brush the dirt from his clothes.

"I think you need to take it easy," Officer Jenkins said, steadying Lucas as he staggered a bit.

"I'm . . . I'm fine," Lucas managed. Talking made his split lip bleed again and he swiped at it again with his hand.

An older lady with short gray hair and carrying what looked like a first aid bag rounded the corner. Spotting Lucas, she hurried toward him, concern on her face.

"Nurse Randolph, this is . . . I didn't get your name," Officer Jenkins said, steering Lucas to an overturned wooden crate he eased him onto.

Lucas tried to take a breath. Even with the slight breeze in the small alley, it was still warm. The air was dusty and smelled of garbage and old food. The school building's solid red brick wall seemed to loom overhead as Lucas sat on the unsteady crate. Leaning over, he put his elbows on his knees, still breathing hard.

Nurse Randolph pulled some cotton gauze and oint-ments from her small bag and began to gently check Lucas' face, hands, and arms for cuts and scrapes.

"Lucas . . . Lucas Matthews," Lucas finally managed to reply to Officer Jenkins' inquiry.

"This is Lucas, Nurse Randolph."

"Yes, I heard," she replied pertly. "Let me see, young man." Nurse Randolph examined the cut on Lucas' lip and then the cut below his left eye.

Lucas painfully flexed his right hand. It was already beginning to swell. He smiled grimly to himself. At least he'd gotten in one good punch. If there was a next time, he wouldn't be caught by surprise.

Nurse Randolph dabbed something onto the cuts, making Lucas wince sharply.

"Hold still," she said, holding Lucas' chin firmly in one hand while she administered the salve.

The salve felt good, but the rest of Lucas ached. This was going to be hard to explain to his new foster dad, whose last words before school that morning had been to stay out of trouble. That had been after he'd slapped Lucas for asking for more breakfast. Lucas shuddered to think what would happen tonight when he went home with a busted lip, a cut, and an accompanying black eye. A swollen hand was going to make things extra tough—writing, doing lessons, or the chores he'd been assigned at home. The damaged clothes weren't going to go over well either.

If only he hadn't stepped in when those three were mistreating a younger girl. Lucas didn't know her, so he'd just watched from a distance, at first. She'd been talking and laughing with the taller, good-looking guy, and they'd seemed to be friends. But, when she tried to walk away, he grabbed her arm. She'd lost her balance and fallen, dropping her books and spilling the papers from her notebook across the floor. Instead of helping her, the three picked up her lunch bag and while laughing, started removing items and tossing them to each other. Lucas could tell the girl was crying, but she'd managed to stand and tried to gather her books and papers while they carelessly walked across them. Lucas knew he couldn't let it pass.

He approached and started helping the girl pick up the scattered papers. He handed them to her before he'd turned to the guys, who were still divvying up the contents from the girl's lunch. He asked them, nicely, to give her lunch back, but they'd turned on him—quickly. They threw the lunch bag aside and before Lucas had a chance to realize what they were about to do, they'd grabbed him and drug him out of the cafeteria's side door and into the alley. It seemed they'd been looking for a fight and liked the three to one odds.

The cafeteria was already mostly empty before classes resumed after lunch, leaving just the girl to know what was happening. Lucas was glad she'd gone for help. She had stayed behind and was now standing to the side, watching anxiously. Lucas tried to give her a reassuring smile but only caused his lip to bleed again.

Nurse Randolph frowned and mumbled, "Tsk, tsk," as she dabbed more salve onto it.

"I think he's going to be fine, Officer Jenkins, but I'll take him back to the nurse's office for the rest of the afternoon and keep an eye on him."

"No, I'm fine. I can go to class," Lucas said as he got to his feet, teetering a bit before he eased back down onto the crate.

"You're going with the nurse," Officer Jenkins said firmly. "I'll call your parents and let them know what's happened. They can pick you up from the nurse's office."

Lucas reflexively cowered. His dread must have shown on his face.

Officer Jenkins looked at him closely. "Is there a problem with calling them, Lucas?"

"Uh, no sir," Lucas said after an uneasy hesitation. "But it's foster parents. I'm new ... here."

He was always new. He'd lost count of how many schools he'd attended, all for short periods of time, before being moved from one foster home to another. Each foster home seemed worse than the one before. This was a new town—an Army base town. He wasn't sure why, but Lucas had hoped Fort Collins would be different than all the other places he'd lived. It felt good to have at least that small connection to another town with an Army base, like where he'd lived with his mom and dad.

Lucas had been in first grade when his dad died. After that, Lucas and his mom had moved around— a lot—and then just a few years later, his mom had died. Lucas would always believe she died from a broken heart. He'd been all alone after that and had been placed into one miserable foster care home after another. He'd lost count of how many or even where he'd lived. It was an ongoing nightmare. All he could do was get through each day and do the best he could. As Mr. Andy had told him: *Sometimes, a lot of times, all you'll have is you. So you gotta be the best you possible.*

This time his foster home was with Jake and Amber Barwood—at least he thought those were their names. He'd only been with them since Friday evening, and it had been a long, miserable weekend, listening to them yell at each other before they turned and started yelling at him. The start of the week at a new school wasn't going too well either. Lucas sighed with dread and resignation.

Officer Jenkins studied Lucas for several long seconds before exchanging a knowing look with Nurse Randolph.

He grasped Lucas' hand and pulled him to his feet before giving him a reassuring pat on the shoulder. He gave Lucas a gentle nudge toward Nurse Randolph with a nod to follow her. Turning, Officer Jenkins looked at the girl who had called for help. "It's time for you to be in class, Meg. Which one is it supposed to be?"

Meg grimaced. "Algebra."

"Ah . . . I can understand your reluctance. Why don't I walk with you for some moral support?" Officer Jenkins asked with a teasing grin.

Meg laughed and smiled shyly as she turned to Lucas.

"Thank you for what you did," she said, before turning and walking away with Officer Jenkins.

Officer Jenkins glanced over his shoulder and gave Lucas a reassuring nod as Nurse Randolph steered Lucas in behind them. Lucas was surprised. These people were actually nice and seemed to care. He wasn't accustomed to people being nice to him. He liked it.

But then again, evening was coming.

Reaching the nurse's office, Nurse Randolph finished treating the cuts and scrapes she hadn't already tended and then left Lucas to rest on the small cot in the back room. Lucas laid, staring at the acoustic tiled ceiling, while his mind drifted. His body ached. But his soul ached more.

He sat up and moved to the edge of the cot, looking around at the small space. The room was virtually colorless between the cream-colored walls, the white ceiling tiles, and the white paper liner on the plastic cot. Besides the cot where he sat, there was a lone plastic chair and a small storage cabinet area with a sink. A faded print of an old-fashioned doctor with a kind smile holding a stethoscope to a young boy's chest hung on the wall behind the cot. All the other walls were blank. Low voices came from the other side of the closed door, but the room itself was completely silent except for the hum of the florescent lighting and the paper liner rustling beneath him when he moved.

Lucas took a leather wallet out of his pocket. It was one of the last things his mom gave him. He opened it and slipped his fingers between the two folds and pulled out the red construction paper leaf and the picture he'd kept all these years. He'd lost his treasure box somewhere along the way, but he'd managed to hold onto these two things that were most important to him. He fingered the leaf gently, running his fingers over the words – "Mr. Andy" and "Fire Trucks."

Second grade seemed like a dream now, but Mr. Andy, the firefighter, was still very, very real. Officer Jenkins reminded Lucas of Mr. Andy. The two looked nothing alike, but they were both kind. And Officer Jenkins had talked to him just like Mr. Andy had, as if he really mattered. Lucas studied the writing on the leaf closer. He already had it memorized, both the words and how it looked. The smear on the words, he knew, was a tear. Mrs. Garrett had been sad that day. Something had been wrong, but he didn't know what and never found out. It was soon after that day his mom pulled him from school, and they'd moved, again. And it wouldn't be the last time.

Returning the leaf to his wallet, Lucas held up the small, wrinkled picture of Jill Barkley and studied it again as he had so many times before. He wondered where Jill was now. He sure missed her. It would be nice to have a friend.

Lucas sighed. He stood and placed the picture back into the wallet, then slid the wallet back into his pocket. He glanced around again and began pacing the shiny linoleum floor. He stopped abruptly, hearing voices. One angry voice over the others caused him to cringe. The door suddenly banged open and his new foster dad, Jake Barwood, charged into the room, his face fierce with anger. Nurse Randolph anxiously hurried in after him.

"Mr. Barwood, please calm down. Lucas did nothing wrong."

"I was called away from work and told I needed to come to the school. Boy," he said, Jake's breathing heavy as he turned on Lucas and took a menacing step closer, "do you know how much it's costing me to be here and not at work?"

Lucas shrunk as far away from this hulk of a man as he could, stopping only when his back touched the wall.

Jake advanced, rigid with anger, his dark eyes laser-focused on Lucas. A large, muscular man with a bald head and beefy, large hands, he loomed over Lucas threateningly.

Nurse Randolph tried to step between Jake and Lucas, but Jake put an arm out, blocking her.

"This boy is my responsibility," he snarled, turning to look at her before quickly returning his attention to Lucas. "Look at him! A busted lip, cuts, and a black eye! If the state finds out, I could lose the money—"

He stopped abruptly, seeming to realize what he was saying. He turned back to Nurse Randolph, plastering a fake smile on his face.

"I mean . . ." he began in a different tone, patting Lucas roughly on the shoulder.

Lucas winced and tried to move, but Jake put a firm hand on him, holding him in place.

"I believe we know exactly what you mean," a voice from behind Nurse Randolph said.

Officer Jenkins walked around the nurse and stepped between Jake and Lucas, pointedly removing Jake's hand from Lucas' shoulder.

"Officer, sir," Jake began, using the same fake tone he'd just used on Nurse Randolph. The smile on his face faded quickly into a frown when Officer Jenkins moved his hand away from Lucas.

"Officer, this boy is in my care. I'll make sure he causes you no more problems."

"I can assure you, Lucas caused no problems. He came to the aid of another student," Officer Jenkins said, sizing Jake Barwood up and not liking what he saw.

Jake Barwood shuffled his feet nervously under the scrutiny but raised his head defiantly.

"Well, uh, we'd better be going. I need to get back to work," Jake said. He reached for Lucas' collar, pulling him roughly along as they headed out the door.

Lucas' heart pounded, not knowing what was going to happen when they were alone. He stole a quick, frightened glance over his shoulder to see Officer Jenkins and Nurse Randolph watching, worried looks on their faces. Lucas understood. He was worried too.

I T WAS WORSE THAN what Lucas had feared. Jake was furious, not only at being called away from work but also from what he'd perceived as Officer Jenkins talking down to him. Jake had shoved Lucas into his old, dinged up truck and when they'd pulled up to the ratty house where Jake and Amber lived, Jake grabbed Lucas by the collar, half shoving, half pushing him up the steps and into the house.

Amber, Jake's wife, looked up in surprise.

"What are you doing home?" she asked, looking between Jake's furious face and Lucas' pale, frightened one. All too familiar with Jake's temper, she immediately shrank away from him in fear.

"What happened?" she asked, her voice more a frightened whisper.

"This kid," Jake said, pulling Lucas up by his collar, "got into a fight at school. The school called, and I had to leave work to pick him up. It won't happen again."

Jake glared fiercely at Lucas. "Come on."

Lucas thought about trying to get away, but he knew from experience, it would only make things worse. He stumbled down the narrow, cluttered hall, with Jake shoving him roughly along the way. He thrust Lucas through the door of the tiny room they'd given him and slammed the door.

"Turn around and bend over," Jake snarled.

The color drained from Lucas' face. "Wha. . .What?!" he stammered.

"You heard me," Jake said with another shove as he started removing his belt.

"Please, sir. No," Lucas said, backing up. But Jake was too strong for him. He pushed Lucas over the bed and began beating him with the belt. Lucas flinched with every stroke, wanting to beg him to stop but too afraid to say anything or even cry out.

After what seemed like hours, Jake, breathing heavily, finally straightened and began lacing his belt back through his pant loops. Lucas lay motionless on the bed, the backs of his legs and his bottom stinging and burning like fire. He could feel the welts rising.

"Let that be a lesson to you, kid. If there are any more fights at school, you'll get it worse next time." Jake paused and took a big breath as he looked down at Lucas. "And just to make sure the lesson is understood, no supper for you either." Jake yanked the door open and slammed it behind him as he left.

Lucas already knew the Barwoods didn't care about him. They just wanted the monthly payments from the state for his care. The money they received was supposed to be spent for food and clothes for him, but he didn't remember ever getting new clothes from them or any other foster parents. It was either hand-me-downs or thrift store clothes that never fit. As for food, he barely got enough to eat, like this morning, but he'd noticed that the Barwoods had plenty and were eating extremely well.

The pain from the welts on Lucas' back and legs was getting worse, and he moaned slightly as he tried to move. Tears pricked his eyes. But just like all the times before, he couldn't, he wouldn't let himself cry. He felt so alone—so utterly alone.

But then, Mr. Andy's voice came to him, again. *Just when you think you can't feel any lower, Lucas, trust me, there's an even lower point. When you're there, take just one step forward and then another. Before too long that low spot is behind you and you'll come to realize you're stronger and better than before.*

Lucas took a deep, shuddering breath and resolved that—somehow—he would take that next step.

LUCAS EASED INTO HIS desk for first period civics class the next morning. The welts on his back, legs, and bottom made it painful to sit. Afraid of Jake's temper, Amber had waited until after he'd fallen asleep on the couch last night before sneaking some salve into Lucas for the welts. It had helped to ease the burning, but the welts were still painful. In his anger, Jake had also struck Lucas across the back. Lucas hadn't been able to reach those welts with the salve, but in spite of the pain, he was resolved to act like nothing had happened. He'd met men like Jake before and was determined not to let Jake get the better of him.

The pain made it hard to concentrate, but eventually class ended and Lucas joined the wave of students in the hall on their way to the next class. He was suddenly aware of someone walking close and keeping step with him. He glanced up to see Officer Jenkins grinning down at him. Lucas nodded and tried to give him a convincing smile.

A slight frown crossed the officer's face before he said, "Good morning, Lucas. Your day off to a good start?" Officer Jenkins looked closely at Lucas, taking note of his ill-fitting clothing and the stilted way he walked.

"Yes, sir. I suppose so," Lucas said quietly, continuing to walk, his eyes focused ahead of him.

Officer Jenkins continued beside Lucas, greeting students passing on either side of them. Lucas didn't like the attention that Officer Jenkins was bringing as he walked with him.

"What's next on your schedule?" Officer Jenkins asked as Lucas slowed to look both ways at a "t" intersection in the hallway. This being only his second day and in another new school, he wasn't sure which way to go for his geometry class.

"Geometry," Lucas finally stated as the students slipped into doorways and the hall began to empty.

"Ah … math wing is to the left," the officer said and pointed.

"Thanks."

Lucas veered to the left, but Officer Jenkins continued with him and stepped closer.

"Those three guys—the ones that attacked you—they've been sent to an alternative school for several weeks. You don't have to worry about seeing them around any time soon. When they do come back, I'm going to make sure they know I'm keeping an eye on them."

Lucas digested that information as he kept walking. At least that was one less thing to worry about ... for now.

Jenkins waited for Lucas to respond but when he didn't, Jenkins asked, leaning in close so the few students remaining in the hall wouldn't overhear, "Everything go alright after you went home yesterday?"

Lucas' steps faltered. Was this someone actually concerned about him? He wasn't sure what to think about that. Before Lucas could answer, Officer Jenkins stopped, drawing Lucas to a stop beside him. Putting a hand on Lucas' shoulder, he gently turned him to face him. Lucas flinched involuntarily and tried to pull away as Officer Jenkins' hand landed on one of the welts on his back.

Officer Jenkins stiffened.

Unwilling to meet Officer Jenkins' appraising look, Lucas looked down and studied a spot on the hall's linoleum floor.

Putting his hands on his hips, Officer Jenkins frowned as he looked at Lucas.

"I ... uh ... I need to get to class. I don't want to get in trouble for being late," Lucas finally said after a few uncomfortable seconds.

"I tell you what, Lucas. I'll speak to Mr. Fields about class today. Why don't you come with me?"

He took off, walking briskly down the hall, but stopped when Lucas didn't follow. He retraced his steps and stopped in front of Lucas.

"You coming?"

"Am I in trouble, sir?" Lucas asked in barely a whisper. He just couldn't get in trouble again, knowing what would happen.

Officer Jenkins' face softened with understanding. He waited until Lucas looked up.

"No, son, you're not in trouble. Not at all. I'd just like for you to come with me. Okay?"

Thinking about it for several seconds, Lucas finally nodded and walked with Officer Jenkins down a couple of halls, surprised when they ended up at the nurse's office.

Lucas looked up questioningly at Officer Jenkins.

"Nurse Randolph wants to visit with you for a few minutes. I'll wait right here for you. Okay?"

Unsure of what was going on, Lucas could only agree.

It had been about thirty minutes when the door opened and Nurse Randolph stepped outside, closing the door softly behind her. Officer Jenkins stood as soon as the door opened, watching her anxiously. She walked to where Officer Jenkins had been waiting and with a solemn look, sat in the chair next to his.

"Well?" Officer Jenkins asked, resuming his seat.

"I'm afraid you were right. That boy was badly beaten with what must have been a belt. He has welts all up and down his back. He said a lady at the house gave him some salve for his legs, but I treated all of them again and gave him something for the pain. I told him to lay on the cot—on his side, of course—for a while. He was out like a light. I don't think he slept much last night."

Jenkins shook his head in frustration.

"Poor kid. He did nothing wrong yesterday and certainly nothing to warrant this." He took a deep breath. "I'm going to report the abuse and see what I can do about having him removed from that home."

Nurse Randolph nodded. "I agree. I don't think it's safe for him to go back there. He also told me he hasn't eaten since breakfast yesterday morning and that wasn't much. The poor thing doesn't know whether he's more tired or hungry. Being more tired won out this time."

Jenkins stood abruptly and started for the door as Nurse Randolph stood as well.

"This kind of stuff drives me crazy," Officer Jenkins said as he reached the outer office door.

"Kids shouldn't be treated as some loser's punching bag. I've been thinking and have an idea, one I think might be a big help to at least a couple of different parties. Keep Lucas here and get him some lunch, anything he wants. My treat."

"It will be my pleasure," Nurse Randolph said with a relieved smile.

S CHOOL WAS LETTING OUT when Officer Jenkins returned to the nurse's office to find Lucas anxiously pacing beside the cot in the back room. Lucas' head popped up when the door eased open. Officer Jenkins was relieved to see, when he stepped inside, that Lucas looked better and more rested.

"Officer Jenkins, I need to go or I'll be late getting back," Lucas said, starting toward the door.

Officer Jenkins held up a hand.

"You don't have to worry, Lucas. You're not going back to that house again."

Lucas' eyes widened. "What? Really?!"

"Yes, really. Nurse Randolph told me what she found when she examined you this morning. Afterward, I went straight to the agency that handled your placement in that home and told them what was happening. They removed you from there as fast as forms could be completed and submitted,"

Officer Jenkins said. "I just got back from the Barwood residence and let me tell you, it was an absolute pleasure to let them know you won't be coming back. I retrieved all of your belongings. Everything is in my patrol car."

Lucas broke into a hesitant but relieved smile.

"Thank you, sir. Really. Thank you. I didn't know how I was going to face going back there."

Officer Jenkins nodded. "And now you don't have to worry about going back—ever. But tell me how are you feeling—better?" Officer Jenkins asked, eying Lucas closely.

"I'm doing much better, sir. Nurse Randolph was very kind and I believe I have you to thank for lunch today."

Officer Jenkins grinned. "I hope you didn't eat me out of my next paycheck."

Lucas laughed. "No, sir, I didn't. But thank you."

"Oh, you're very welcome, Lucas. But now," Officer Jenkins paused and heaved an exaggerated sigh, "*I* need a favor from *you*."

Lucas frowned, looking puzzled. "A favor from me?"

"Yeah. I'd like for you to meet a good friend of mine."

"Well . . . sure," Lucas agreed with a perplexed shrug.

Officer Jenkins stepped to the door and gave Lucas an encouraging smile before gesturing to someone to enter.

A slender man of medium height with an athletic build stepped inside. His face was tan with ruddy cheeks and he looked like he spent a lot of time outdoors. His dark brown hair was short and his green eyes were kind, but a bit wary, when he looked at Lucas. He offered a hesitant smile as he continued shuffling the baseball cap he held through his fingers.

Grinning, Officer Jenkins gave Lucas a conspiratorial nod. "Lucas Matthews, I'd like to introduce you to Craig Holmes. Craig this is Lucas Matthews."

Lucas stuck his hand out just as his dad had taught him to do when meeting someone. "Good afternoon, sir," Lucas said firmly, looking Mr. Holmes directly in the eye.

The man nodded slightly as he took Lucas' hand, shaking it firmly and returning Lucas' direct look.

"It's a real pleasure to meet you, Lucas," Mr. Holmes said. He looked at Officer Jenkins and seemed to relax before looking back to Lucas to study the confident, mannerly young man in front of him.

Lucas looked uncertainly between the two, not sure what was going on.

"Lucas," Officer Jenkins began, placing his hand lightly on Lucas' shoulder, "I've told Mr. Holmes and his wife, Patsy, about you and your situation. They would like you to come and live with their family. Would you like that?"

Lucas had never been given a choice before. He hesitated, unsure of what to say.

Mr. Holmes pulled up a chair and motioned for Lucas to sit on the edge of the cot across from him. Lucas eased down, still mindful of the painful welts as Mr. Holmes took a seat in the chair.

"Lucas, I think it's only fair to tell you about my family before you agree to anything. We've been through a lot. And from what Officer Jenkins has told me, you have too. So I get it if you may not want to take on any more right now. Will you give me ten minutes for us to talk?" Mr. Holmes asked.

Lucas looked at the clock and nodded. Officer Jenkins stepped outside and pulled the door closed softly behind him.

"Lucas," Mr. Holmes began, "my wife, Patsy and I have—I mean, had—two children: Avery and Meg. Meg is in eighth grade here at Baker Heights. You may know her. And our son, Avery . . . well, Avery died from an accidental Fentanyl overdose a year ago." Tears filled Mr. Holmes' kind eyes as he looked away.

Self-consciously clearing his throat, Mr. Holmes looked back to Lucas and continued. "We still miss him terribly but know he would want us to figure out a way to go on. We believe we have a lot to share with the right young man who would like to join our family. From what Officer Jenkins has told me and from our brief meeting just now, both he, and now I, believe you are the right young man and would be a great addition to our home. I only thought it was right that you know our story since our family is still grieving. We would love for you to join our home. But you, of course, should have a say in the matter too. If you decide against it, there are no worries. Other suitable arrangements and in a safe place will be made for you. I'll leave you alone for a few minutes so you can think about it. Okay?"

Stunned at this sudden turn of events, Lucas could only nod.


Lucas stared at the door after Mr. Holmes walked out and closed it behind him. The bare walls of the room and even the florescent lights seemed brighter as hope began to seep in—hope he hadn't felt in a long time. He was being given a choice. Was it possible Mr. Holmes and his family were as nice as he certainly seemed to be? Could this be the end of bouncing from house to house, always being the new kid at school, being mistreated by those who only wanted money? Lucas dared a small smile. This could be a whole new life for him, something he'd dreamed of having.

But then again, dreams could turn into nightmares. He had enough scars and bruises to prove it.

He'd made up his mind.

He stood slowly, painfully but walked with

determination to the door. He took a deep breath and put his hand on the knob, opening the door and stepping through. Mr. Andy had told him one time, *If there's something you really want to do and you feel it's truly the right thing, tell yourself you can do it. Stick to it because you know you can. And then, see it through.*

Lucas was ready to take on whatever lay on the other side.

OFFICER JENKINS CHATTED AMIABLY on the drive to Mr. Holmes' house. Lucas was glad. For the first time, he was nervous about meeting a new foster family. It had never mattered to him before. He always knew he'd probably be there only for a short time but this time…this seemed more promising. He actually felt hopeful. But then, he did his best to tamp that unusual feeling down. He had to meet the family first. It still might not work out.

Officer Jenkins pulled his patrol car into the drive and parked behind Mr. Holmes' car. Lucas eyed the house with wonder. It was a two-story house—not large but nice. The lawn was manicured, the grass a rich green. The flower beds were neat and lined with a border of brightly colored flowers with green shrubs right behind. A large tree on either side of the house seemed to frame the setting like a picture. It *looked* like a real family lived here.

Officer Jenkins watched Lucas with a smile as he took it all in.

Mr. Holmes walked to the front door and waited, while Officer Jenkins and Lucas retrieved Lucas' things from the back of the patrol car. He didn't have much.

They each carried a small bag as they made their way up the walk. Mr. Holmes opened the door and stepped inside, calling for his wife and daughter. Lucas followed Officer Jenkins through the door into a small entry and then a cozy family room. Lucas immediately felt like he'd come home. The room was lined with deep honey-colored paneling. Strong beams of the same color were overhead as a ceiling fan turned slowly. Two walls held built-in cabinets filled with books and a collection of family pictures. Another wall was the backdrop for two chairs and a small table with a lamp glowing warmly between them. Directly across from the entry was a sliding glass door with windows on either side, overlooking a covered patio that held a large grill and a picnic table. A fireplace was on the fourth wall and a big screen TV hung above the mantel. A brown leather sectional filled the room, with a square leather covered foot stool in the middle.

Lucas self-consciously took everything in. He'd never seen a house like this before and was acutely aware how out of place he looked, standing in the middle of the room wearing jeans that were too short, a shirt that had more than one hole and scuffed up shoes that were too small for his feet. The possibility of living here was just too good to be true.

"Lucas?" Mr. Holmes said as he stepped from the kitchen into the family room. He was followed by who must be his wife. And behind her was the girl Lucas had defended at school. Her eyes grew wide at the sight of him as his did, seeing her.

Mrs. Holmes dropped her husband's hand and walked hesitantly to Lucas, enveloping him in a loose hug.

"Lucas, welcome to our home. Now your home. I hope you like it. I know we're glad you're here," she said with a timid smile.

Lucas returned her smile. He recognized the signs of grief on her face. It was the same look he'd seen on his mother's face after his dad's death. Patsy Holmes was a petite, very pretty woman with dark hair and bright hazel eyes. In spite of the sadness Lucas could see in her eyes, she seemed to genuinely be happy to have Lucas with them.

"Lucas!" Meg, their daughter, said and walked over and hugged him tentatively. "Thank you for coming to my rescue the other day. Looks like you're not only my hero but you're going to be my big brother too!"

Meg looked a lot like her mother, petite with dark hair, but her eyes were her father's green eyes. Where Meg's eyes seemed to spark and flash, Mr. Holmes' eyes were gentle and kind.

Mr. and Mrs. Holmes exchanged a sad look at what Meg had said. Meg seemed oblivious to the pain her parents still felt at her brother's loss, but Lucas understood.

Lucas couldn't help but blush and grin when Meg called him a hero. He'd been called a lot of things but never a hero. Maybe this really was a brand-new start.

"I can't thank you enough," Lucas began, turning to the Holmes, wanting, but knowing he was failing to convey how much a welcome into their family and into their beautiful and loving home meant to him.

Officer Jenkins set Lucas' bags on the floor, just inside the door, and turned to leave.

"I'll be leaving now. Want to let all of you get acquainted. I look forward to seeing you at school, Lucas," Office Jenkins said with a happy glint in his eye. "I'm so happy for you," he added softly to Lucas and then louder to everyone, "I'm happy for all of you."

Before he realized what he was doing, Lucas walked quickly to Officer Jenkins and hugged him tightly.

"Thank you, sir. Thank you." It was all Lucas could manage.

Officer Jenkins patted Lucas lightly on the back as tears welled in his eyes. He looked toward the Holmes, whose eyes shone with tears as well. But this time, they were happy tears.

Officer Jenkins cleared his throat and patted Lucas on the shoulder. "I hope you like football," he said with a grin.

Lucas' brows arched in question as he looked between the Holmes and Officer Jenkins.

"Coach Holmes is the head high school football coach, just so you know," Officer Jenkins said with a wink.

Lucas eyed his new foster dad, his foster mother and yes, even a new foster sister with wonder. This *really* was all just too good to be true.

THE NEXT SEVERAL MONTHS flew by. And then a year. And then another year flew by. So much had happened. Even after living with the Holmes for two years, Lucas still couldn't believe it was real, not after experiencing so many tough years before. He had an actual home where he was part of a real family and . . . loved.

They had all decided, together, that Lucas would call his foster parents Coach and Patsy. He could never call anyone else mom besides his real mom. Patsy had taken him shopping for clothes when he first came to live with them. He wasn't crazy about the actual shopping, but she'd bought him an entire new wardrobe with clothes that actually fit and kept adding clothes as he outgrew things. Thanks to the new clothes, he felt a wave of unfamiliar—but welcome—self-confidence.

The Holmes didn't talk about their son, Avery, very much. Lucas didn't like to talk about his mom either, so he understood. Lucas had heard through talk at school that Avery had taken some medicine that had been laced with Fentanyl and died from an overdose. For such a loving family, Lucas knew that loss had to have been especially hard.

They'd closed off Avery's room for now so Lucas had been given the guest room. He'd gotten to decide how to decorate it—another first for him. He loved the big double bed that had a nightstand and reading lamp on either side. The bedspread was a crisp navy blue, trimmed in white, with matching curtains on the window that overlooked the backyard. A large navy blue bean bag in one corner was where Lucas kicked back with a good book or an occasional video game. A banker's lamp pooled a warm puddle of light in the center of his desk where his laptop, notebook, books from school, and other items were all in easy reach. Several football posters intermingled with copies of family photos Patsy insisted be hung in Lucas' room. Sports trophies from both little league and junior high lined the room's shelves. This was Lucas' own special haven, something he'd never had before. And he loved it.

Avery had been just a little older than Lucas when he'd died, and the pictures in the family room when Lucas first moved in were of a happy, smiling family. Coach and Patsy hadn't looked the same as they had in those pictures but now, their lighthearted smiles seemed to have returned and pictures on the family room shelves now included Lucas. When they'd asked if he'd like to be in their official Christmas family portrait, Lucas had been especially pleased.

The Holmes had understandably been distant at first but they'd gradually relaxed and began treating Lucas like a son. He had been cautious to let his guard down around them at first as well. But now, there was easy laughter, good-natured teasing, and even some occasional family-style yelling around the house.

Becoming part of a real family had opened doors Lucas never even knew existed, and he began to excel in his studies. Having to move so often, Lucas' grades hadn't been good. He hadn't really cared. But now, all of that had changed, and Lucas wanted to do well on his schoolwork. The Holmes hired some high school students who were tutors in subjects where Lucas hadn't done well or was behind. He'd never been a straight-A student, but he was gaining steady ground as he headed into his senior year. His favorite subject was science, and he'd joined the Science Club. The guys on the football team gave him a hard time and called him a science geek, but he didn't care. He was fascinated by science and how chemicals and the elements worked together. He just couldn't get enough and looked forward to every class, lab, and experiment. Lucas also knew having a strong working knowledge of materials, their composition, and how chemicals and materials interacted with one another would be useful when he became a firefighter.

Having a little sister was a new experience for Lucas as well. And even though she could be annoying at times, he had to admit he rather liked having Meg around. He wasn't sure if he was just more aware of things because of how he'd grown up, but he wondered if all girls were as unaware of the bad influences and bad actors out there as Meg seemed to be. Lucas had a constant, nagging feeling that he needed to be extra mindful and look out for her. The two were friends, even confidants, and as a big brother he realized he was willing to do anything to look out for and protect her.

It had been a time of adjustment for all of them, but now, their family functioned fully as a cohesive unit. Lucas still couldn't believe he'd found such a wonderful home with a family who really loved and cared for him. A family that he loved and cared for just as much in return.

COACH LOOKED AROUND HIS office at the field house. The smells of leather, soap, and cleaning disinfectant filled the air, as did the muffled voices of dozens of eager young men in the locker room on the other side of the door. Coach looked out the large window that overlooked the practice field. He loved this sport and adored working with these young men. It had been a great preseason and with the school year getting underway in the next couple of days, he knew they were anxious to get the football season underway as well.

He scanned the list he held in his hand of players selected for the varsity team. He smiled when he saw Lucas' name as running back. He knew Lucas should have been on varsity last year but not many juniors made the varsity team. He'd talked to Lucas about it and they'd agreed Lucas would stay back and play on the junior varsity team one more year, just to avoid people thinking that the coach was showing partiality.

Coach shook his head, thinking of Lucas. What a kid. He got along with everyone and was always so agreeable. Well, correct that—he got along with *almost* everyone. Joel De Grey and his two friends, Marty Pierce and Tony Harlow, were the exceptions. But they really didn't count. Those three were so cocky and sure of themselves, no one else cared to be around them either. Coach knew they were the ones who'd jumped Lucas in middle school and there still seemed to be some bad blood on the part of De Grey and his pals. With the four now playing on the same football team, he and the other coaches would need to be extra vigilant to make sure everything stayed under control.

Coach almost jumped when a sharp knock came at the door.

"Enter," he said, standing and slipping his whistle around his neck.

One of the assistant coaches, Coach Morgan, opened the door and stuck his head inside. "They're ready if you are, Coach," he said with a quick nod before stepping back out and closing the door.

Coach Holmes picked up his playbook and notes and started toward the door. A new high school football season was underway.

—

Two years. Lucas had been team manager for the Fort Collins High School varsity team for two years. He'd picked wet towels up off the floor. He'd filled water bottles and held them up to squeeze water into the mouths of thirsty varsity players. He'd picked up practice gear, cleaning it and stowing it. He'd done the laundry, washing loads every day after practice. He'd packed and hauled equipment before and after every game. He'd paid his dues. And now, he was a full-fledged member of the varsity team and happy to be on the team with so many of his closest friends.

He and Evan Wright, this year's team manager, had worked for most of the day yesterday in anticipation of having everything ready for the team's first practice. Lucas had patiently shown Evan how to set the locker room up, training him on how and what needed to be done before and after each practice and how to adjust the routine for games.

Each locker had a player's name stenciled at the top with a faded practice jersey hanging on an old wire clothes hanger. For games, a bright crimson jersey would hang in each locker instead. Each player's pants were neatly folded and on the shelf underneath the jersey while cleats, like the pants according to size, sat neatly in front of each locker. Extra hangers hung in each locker for street clothes and a bottle of water sat next to the pants.

With it being his senior year and first year on varsity, Lucas was especially pleased to see a locker of his own with its number 27 practice jersey hanging inside, everything neat and ready just for him.

All was in order. As they looked around at the end of the day, Lucas had given Evan a fist bump, pleased, as they surveyed the room. The locker room looked great.

LUCAS HAD JOINED IN the boisterous laughter and good-natured shoves among his teammates as they waited for Coach's start of season speech, but he stepped away quietly to double-check and make sure Evan was all situated and everything was good to go in the locker room.

He moved between the first row of lockers that were designated for the defense, and everything looked great. Pleased, he smiled to himself. But when he came around the edge of the row of lockers into the area designated for the offense, he froze mid step. Every locker and everything in the area was in perfect order except . . . except for his locker. His practice jersey, along with his pants, socks—everything—had been wadded up and thrown onto the bottom shelf. His cleats lay on top, with dirt generously thrown all over the pile, muddy from the water poured out of the discarded water bottle rocking back and forth on the bench.

Lucas' breath hitched as he took a tentative step toward the mess.

"Lucas, come on, Coach is about to—" Nate saw Lucas staring silently at the shambles of his locker. "What happened?"

Nate stood beside Lucas who fingered the soiled jersey.

"Come on, guys, we're—" Coach Morgan said. He let out a low whistle.

Curious as to what was holding them up, Coach Holmes also stepped into the locker area. Seeing Lucas and the condition of his locker, Coach's jaw clenched. The rest of the team silently joined them to stand behind Coach.

"Whoever is responsible for this, please be aware that this is school property," Coach said looking around the room, his gaze landing on Joel, Marty, and Tony. "You'll be paying for these damages. Evan, get Matthews here a whole new set of gear and clean up the locker. This, gentlemen, is unacceptable behavior, and when I find out the responsible party, or parties, you will be removed from the team. Period. No questions asked."

Lucas stepped back as Evan moved in beside him with cleaning supplies, another practice jersey, and set up. When Lucas turned to follow Coach and the rest of the team, he caught the gleeful stares of Joel, Marty, and Tony.

"Wow, Matthews. Tough luck," Joel said in a low voice with a snicker as Marty and Tony chuckled. "Looks like you've got an enemy, or enemies, on the team. You really should be careful. But you know, who could blame them?" Joel laughed, then quickly sobered as Coach walked up behind him.

"You know something about this, De Grey?" Coach asked, narrowing his eyes as he looked between the three.

"Us? Oh, no sir. Of course not. Can't imagine who would do such a thing. And to single out Matthews here? Well, it just doesn't make any sense does it?" Joel said, feigning seriousness.

Coach stared intensely at Joel for several more seconds before turning and heading back toward the meeting space to get things started. Nate swung an arm around Lucas' neck as some of the other players reached over and gave Lucas a friendly shove or a pat on the back as they followed Coach.

Joel De Grey grunted as he hit the ground after a hard hit from Chad Bloom. Exuding kindness, Bloom reached down to give Joel a hand up, but instead of letting go, he pulled Joel close to where they were nose guard to nose guard. Other linemen, defense and offense, gathered behind Bloom, staring icily at De Grey.

Clinching De Grey's jersey in his hands, Bloom lifted De Grey a fraction off the ground.

"De Grey, this is a simple word of warning but hear it well. If you ever, *ever* even think of doing something like that little locker stunt again or anything else to Matthews, be aware you'll have us to answer to," Bloom said through gritted teeth as the others moved a threatening step closer.

"And that goes for your buddies too," Bloom added, looking over Joel's shoulder pads at Marty and Tony.

Joel coughed and sputtered an incoherent reply but finally nodded reluctantly when Bloom lifted him even further off the ground.

"Good. So long as we're clear." Bloom dropped De Grey into a heap on the ground as the offense, and most of the defense, trotted off leaving De Grey, Marty, and Tony behind.

"What was all that about?" Lucas asked as they joined him on the sidelines for a water break.

Bloom shrugged. "Nothing really. Just making sure we were clear on some communication issues."

Lucas looked around the circle. Most of his teammates were trying to hide grins as they took their turn drinking some water. Lucas had a feeling there was a lot more to it than that.

So Meg, I think with that one minor change to your schedule, you're all set. Senior high is a big change, but you've got some great teachers. You know, I can't believe you're already a sophomore. I remember when you were born!" Mrs. Thompson, the high school guidance counselor, said, sweeping her cat-framed glasses from her nose. Mrs. Thompson had been at Fort Collins Senior High for forever, Meg thought, as she handed Meg the approved final schedule for her sophomore year.

Meg smiled indulgently. She had heard the same remark from multiple teachers and now, her guidance counselor. Sometimes, it was a good thing to be the football coach's daughter and knowing most of the high school staff growing up. And then, other times not so much.

"Thank you, Mrs. Thompson," Meg said, standing and picking up her notebook. "I appreciate that and I'm excited to finally be here. I'll be in touch if I have any questions."

Mrs. Thompson nodded distractedly as she tapped some keys on her keyboard. She smiled at Meg and looked to the clock, before calling the next student in line into her office.

Meg looked at her schedule as she walked out of the office and joined her friends, Bethany, Margo, and Kit, in the busy hallway. The glass in the office door rattled slightly as the door closed behind Meg.

"Let's compare," Kit said. All four looked at their schedules, naming off classes and teachers for each class period.

"Well, at least we've got a few classes together. I guess we couldn't expect to have them all," Meg said. They each sighed in agreement. They put their notebooks away and took a few steps down the hall before stopping and continuing to talk as they huddled in a loose circle close to the wall.

Their busy chatter was interrupted when a boy Meg vividly remembered from middle school walked up and casually joined them. The girls made room for him as he eyed each of them before his gaze landed on Meg.

"Sophomores, I take it?" he said smoothly. "Let me be the first to welcome you to Fort Collins Senior High. My name is Joel De Grey. And yours?" he asked, looking to each as they replied, starting with Margo. "Oh, and these are my friends. Guys." He waved two large guys forward. "Marty Pierce and Tony Harlow."

The group began a stilted conversation as Joel turned to Meg and said quietly, "You look familiar. Have we met before?"

Meg looked in eyes so dark they almost seemed to match the black of his dark wavy hair. He was several inches taller than her and well built. He'd gotten better looking since middle school ... much better-looking. Meg blushed under his scrutiny.

"Yes ... we were at Baker Heights Middle School together. My name is Meg Holmes."

"Ah, I thought so," he smiled pleasantly. "Your Coach Holmes' daughter I believe?"

Meg nodded bashfully.

"Well Meg, hopefully we'll be seeing a lot more of each other around school. I look forward to that."

The conversation had died down and Joel's final comment was heard by the entire group. It was met with giggles and wide eyes from Meg's friends.

Joel smiled as if he'd expected their reaction.

"I'll see you soon ... Meg," Joel said as he and his two friends sauntered away and joined the throng of students in the hall.

"Meg! He's gorgeous!" Margot said, turning to watch them walk down the hall.

"And a senior!" Kit said wide-eyed. "You gotta go for that, girl!"

Surprised but pleased to have received attention from such a guy, Meg couldn't help but smile. She glanced up and saw Lucas and his closest friend, Nate Flowers, approaching from the other direction.

"Lucas!" Meg called out when she saw him.

Margot shook her head and smiled. "You know, some girls have all the luck. A good-looking guy singles you out before school even starts *and* you've got an incredibly cute brother. It's just not fair."

Everyone laughed as Margot stuck her bottom lip out playfully.

Lucas and Nate managed to navigate through a crowd of what were evidently sophomores, searching the rows of lockers on either side of the hall for their locker. Lucas and Nate exchanged indulgent grins as they finally reached Meg and her friends.

"What's not fair?" Lucas asked with a grin as he and Nate walked up.

Margot turned bright red as the other two girls giggled loudly.

Lucas and Nate looked at each other, confused.

"What? What did I say?" Lucas asked, perplexed.

"Oh, they're just jealous," Meg replied.

"Jealous of what?" Lucas pressed, a frown furrowing his forehead.

"They're jealous of me because..." Meg paused as Margot, Kit and Bethany turned and suddenly hurried away.

Nate shook his head. "Do you always have that effect on girls, Matthews?"

Lucas shrugged. "I didn't think so but..."

Meg laughed. "You *do* have that affect, Lucas. They all think you're 'incredibly cute,'" she said, doing the air quotes with a teasing grin.

"Hey, Lucas! You're 'incredibly cute,'" Nate said, laughing and mimicking Meg's air quotes.

Lucas blushed. He chuckled, giving Nate a good-natured shove. "Cut it out..."

"And," Meg went on, her eyes sparkling, "I'll have you know, I just had an 'incredibly cute' upper-class-man come over and say hi. He said he hopes to see more of me around school. Senior high is already looking good. So, what do you think about that?"

"Well, I guess that depends," Lucas said, crossing his arms across his chest as he studied his little sister. "Who is this upper-class-man?"

Meg twirled a strand of her brown hair in her fingers. "Now, don't be pulling the big brother thing on me, Lucas Matthews. You know him so it's no big deal. It's Joel De Grey. Remember him from middle school? He..."

Meg stopped short when she saw the look that crossed Lucas' face.

"Stay away from him, Meg," Lucas said, leaning down and looking her intently in the eye. "Promise me, please. Just stay away from him. He's trouble."

Meg frowned. "Well, he seems really nice to me. I remember he was a jerk in middle school, but he seems different now. He was really nice. Come on, Lucas, don't worry about it. I'm in senior high now. I need to stretch my wings a bit."

"Meg, please," Lucas said again. But he was interrupted by several of his friends and other members of the football team walking up.

Lucas turned back to say something to Meg, but she was already gone. Lucas sighed. He needed to stop this before it got started. He pulled out his phone to send Meg a quick text to call her back.

"You coming, Matthews?" Cory Peters asked as the group started to leave. "We're headed for burgers."

Lucas looked at his phone, his fingers ready to type, and then down the hall. He couldn't spot Meg among the groups of students filling the hall.

"Yeah. Coming," he said with a last glance, shaking his head and sliding his phone back into his pocket.

THE SECOND WEEK OF school was winding down and things were settling into a routine for Lucas. The days were long and full of activity, from football practice early in the morning before school while temperatures remained hot, to classes and his science club activities. His job at Auto Works was keeping him busy the remaining hours of the day. He only got to see Meg in passing until late one afternoon, on a rare day when practice was called off early because of the heat Meg found him in his room, studying.

"Lucas," Meg began and waited impatiently for him to acknowledge her. "Lucas, will you take me to the mall?"

Lucas still didn't look up from his book.

"Lucas, come on. You promised you'd take me when I wanted to go. Remember?" Meg wheedled, giving Lucas a playful shove.

"Yeah, yeah, I remember. I will a little later, but I've got to study right now," Lucas said, trying to focus on his science book, fully aware Meg was inches away, bouncing impatiently on her toes.

"Dad said I can go to the store but only if you drive me. Pleeeeaaaaaassse! I want to go shopping," she said, using her best begging voice. She knew Lucas would do anything she asked—it just took a little coaxing.

"I told Felicia we'd pick her up and she said her mom will pick us up afterward."

Lucas ran his fingers through his hair and rolled his eyes. He gazed at Meg as he looked up from his book and the clutter on his desk he'd planned to clean up this afternoon. He had to admit for a little sister, she really was pretty, with her long dark hair and the bright green eyes that were looking at him so imploringly. He knew he was probably overly protective, but he had his reasons—valid reasons. Actually, three of them.

Lucas had hoped after the first of school that Joel De Grey would leave Meg alone, but Joel was relentless and seemed to have a keen interest in Meg. With De Grey constantly hanging around, that meant Marty and Tony were never far away. Lucas cringed just thinking of them.

He couldn't understand Meg's interest in De Grey, especially after the way he'd treated her in middle school. When he'd asked her about it once, she'd said something about Joel being 'dreamy'—whatever that meant—and that he was being really nice to her. As far as Lucas could tell from being around him and his cohorts at football practice, none of the three had improved. He couldn't put his finger on exactly what it was, but there was something about the three that gave Lucas a bad feeling. He ran interference as much as he could, but De Grey was persistent. And knowing Meg, Lucas was afraid that pushing too hard would only encourage her in De Grey's direction.

"Well? Are you going to take me?" Meg asked again, bringing Lucas back to her impatient cajoling. He sighed. He really didn't mind driving her and her friends around—he just didn't let Meg know that. Her friends still giggled a lot when he was around, which was a bit annoying. Meg said it was just because they were nervous around him, but Lucas couldn't figure out why they'd be nervous.

"Lucas? Are you even listening to me?" Meg whined, flouncing down on his bed, causing the springs to squeak loudly. She crossed her arms in front of her, her bottom lip protruding in a frown.

Lucas leaned back in his chair, biting the cap of his pen, studying Meg with a teasing grin.

"Shopping, huh? You've got two or three of everything. What else could you possibly need?" he asked with mock irritation.

Meg sighed dramatically. "I want to go to the cosmetics store. Felicia and I want to see if there are any new nail polish colors."

Lucas rolled his eyes. "Nail polish? Seriously? You two want me to drive you all the way to the mall just for nail polish?"

Meg rolled her eyes at him in frustration.

He glanced at the clock on his nightstand, then back to Meg. He really did need to study for that test, but he couldn't resist Meg either.

"Okay, I'll take you. I'll text Nate to see what he's doing. He and I can hang out at the food court while you and Felicia shop. But then I've got to get back to study."

Meg squealed, jumped up and gave him a hug and quick kiss on the cheek. "But you don't have to wait for me. Felicia's mom said she'd bring us home."

Lucas shook his head. "Nope. I'll wait for you. Now get ready so we can go and get back."

"Okay...Okay. I'll be right back."

Lucas picked up his pen and went back to studying. He knew from experience that Meg could take thirty minutes to an hour getting ready. He grinned. He had plenty of time to knock out a chapter or two.

Lucas checked his phone for the third time in five minutes, looking for a reply text from Meg. He glanced across the wide expanse of the mall's food court for any sign of

Meg or Felicia. Meg was supposed to have met him here fifteen minutes ago.

The food court wasn't crowded, which made it easy for Lucas to see down the four halls of shops that spoked from it. Meg was nowhere in sight.

"She'll be here. Don't sweat it," Nate Flowers said, taking a bite of his fourth taco.

"Sure, that's easy for you to say," Lucas said, taking a drink of his soda and looking around once more. "Your little sister isn't crazy over Joel De Grey."

Nate nodded as he crunched some tortilla chips. "Yeah, you've got a point," he said through a mouthful. Nate picked up his drink and then froze, looking over Lucas' left shoulder.

"What? What is it?" Lucas asked, turning to look and then freezing too.

It was Meg. She was taking her time, casually strolling down the main hallway that intersected with the food court. She didn't see Lucas, or Nate, not that she was looking for them. She only had eyes for Joel De Grey, who was walking beside her and casually putting his hand on her shoulder while he talked. When he did, he grinned down into Meg's face, causing her to blush and then start giggling.

Eyes trained on the two, Lucas stood abruptly and started toward them, Nate quickly on his heels.

Glancing up, a look of triumph crossed Joel's face when he saw Lucas and Nate approaching.

"Matthews, Flowers, what an unexpected pleasure. Meg and I were just ..."

"You and Meg were just nothing," Lucas said, stepping between them, forcing Joel to take a step back.

"Lucas! Come on," Meg said. "We were just ..."

"Where's Felicia?" Lucas asked, cutting Meg off.

Meg huffed and crossed her arms in front of her with no reply.

"No matter," Lucas said, stepping to the side and blocking Joel from getting close to Meg. "It's time to go home."

"Home? Come on, Matthews. Get serious," Joel mocked. "It's not your real home now is it? Just like *she's* not your real sister."

It wasn't unusual for Joel to go out of his way to single Lucas out at school to taunt and ridicule him, but it *was* unusual for him to do it in front of Meg. Joel, for whatever reason, loved to bring attention to the fact that Lucas was a foster kid and not the Holmes' real son. While technically true, hearing someone like De Grey continually bringing it up, wore on Lucas and it hurt him now seeing the distressed look Joel's remark had brought to Meg's face.

"Oh, Lucas," she said with a gasp, stepping closer to him. "I'm sorry. Felicia's mom picked her up. I ran into Joel on the way to the food court and he said he'd walk with me to find you."

"How kind of him," Lucas replied with a look in Joel's direction. He turned to Meg. "Come on, let's go."

Joel started to take a threatening step toward Lucas, but Nate stepped up and shook his head. "Don't even think about it, De Grey."

Joel stepped back, looking angrily between Lucas and Nate.

"I'll see you around, Meg," Joel said with a wink. He turned to Lucas and Nate. "And the same to you boys. It will especially be a pleasure to see you around sometime, Matthews. Alone."

Lucas nodded solemnly. Without saying a word, he took Meg's arm, turned, and walked toward the exit where he'd parked, stepping around a group of diners who had just emerged from one of the restaurants located on the edge of the food court area.

"Lucas, I'm so sorry," Meg said, with a quick glance over her shoulder to Joel, her chin quivering. "What he said . . ."

"Ah, don't worry about it. I don't. He's said worse." Lucas tried to laugh but it didn't quite come out that way.

Nate clapped Lucas on the shoulder and gave him an encouraging smile as they pushed the door open and walked into the heat outside.

THE AUGUST SUN IN Texas continued to be relentlessly brutal. Sweat dripped from Lucas' nose and onto his already sweat-soaked jersey. He scuffed his cleat on the practice field's scorched turf, raising a puff of dust as waves of heat shimmered across the field.

The call from the huddle was a run and the ball was to go to Lucas. When the ball was snapped, Trevor Singletary, team captain and quarterback, handed the ball off to Lucas. Lucas had made it past the line of scrimmage, dust and sweat flying all around him, when he was hit and hit hard from behind. He went down immediately and landed on top of the ball with a resounding thud. The impact knocked the breath out of him. He landed face down, gasping for air, his helmet guard deep in the dry grass and dirt.

"Get used to it, Matthews," Lucas heard Tony Harlow hiss in his ear before other excited voices gathered around them. Lucas struggled and managed to get to one knee, holding the ball up. Joel, Marty, and Tony's eyes narrowed angrily as Lucas met their glare with a challenging grin.

"Matthews! You okay, man?" Trevor asked, clapping Lucas on his shoulder pads, and steering him back toward the huddle after giving him a hand up. "Those guys are relentless. What's their deal today?"

"I don't think they like my charming personality," Lucas said, spitting grass out of his mouth.

Trevor chuckled. "I'm passing the word to the offensive line to give them a little more of the direct business, if you know what I mean. Somebody, and right now it looks like you, is going to get hurt if they don't dial it back a bit."

Lucas nodded as he stepped into the huddle and bent over, putting his hands on his knees, trying to catch his breath.

The scrimmage between offense and defense continued to be physically tough, and not just from the heat, but from the intensity. Coach had given the defense several warnings and reminded them they were all on the same team.

After taking several especially hard hits, Lucas knew he was going to be extra sore tomorrow. It seemed the defensive line had a score to settle, and Lucas was more often their target than not.

"Come on, Lucas," Chad Bloom chided irritably, "just let us give them one really hard, I mean *really hard* hit. They're coming after you on just about every play. It's just not right and we're tired of it."

Several other offensive players nodded in agreement as they stood in a loose circle on one side of the field, taking a water break.

Lucas squeezed in a mouthful of water from a bottle before spitting it onto the parched grass. Lucas held the water bottle in one hand and his helmet in the other, fisted and resting on his hip. His entire body ached.

"I appreciate it, guys, but practice is almost over. Just let it ride. Because if we do that, they're only going to come after everybody harder. We do have a season to play, you know? And maybe, if we're lucky, they'll take some of their anger out on the offense of some other team."

Frustrated head shakes and protests went around the circle, but Lucas waved them off with a tired grin as he handed his water bottle back to Evan.

"Come on, let's end practice on *our* terms," Lucas said, a knowing glint in his eye.

When they lined up, Joel smirked at Lucas as he took his stance across the line. Trevor made the call and Joel exploded off the line, not going for the ball but for Lucas, pummeling him to the ground then landing heavily on top of him.

Lucas grunted with the impact. But then he smiled into De Grey's red, sweat-streaked face.

"That all ya got?" Lucas asked softly as Joel started to stand.

Joel stiffened, then started toward Lucas as Chad gave Lucas a hand up. The offense and some others on the defense, who didn't seem too keen on the direction things were headed, gathered behind Lucas, exchanging glares with Joel, Marty, and Tony.

Shoves were exchanged, with Joel grabbing Lucas' jersey and pulling him in close. Joel's facemask struck Lucas' helmet with a jolt.

"Don't tempt me, Matthews," he hissed, where only Lucas could hear. "You don't know what a hit really is, but you're about to find out."

Lucas just smiled and patted Joel on the shoulder pads. He wasn't going to give Joel De Grey the pleasure of getting the better of him. Not now and—if he could help it—not ever.

As Lucas started to step away, De Grey grabbed his arm and butted into him forcefully with his shoulder pads.

Seeing how the situation was developing, Coach and several of the assistant coaches headed toward the players from the sidelines with quick strides. Coach had watched the hits Lucas had been taking all afternoon. He should have stepped in and stopped it before now, but Lucas had made it clear, he didn't want it to look like the Coach was playing favorites. But now, Coach was putting a stop to things before they really got out of hand.

Reaching Lucas and De Grey, Coach stepped between them and pushed them apart.

"De Grey, I've warned you about these kinds of hits already today," Coach said, his eyes fierce. "Knock it off or you'll sit out the rest of practice. Or maybe even a game or two if you can't keep your temper in check."

De Grey jerked loose from the Coach's grasp and started back toward the defense's huddle, mumbling something under his breath.

Coach's head jerked around, hearing what De Grey had said. Coach quickly followed De Grey and yanked him out of the defensive huddle.

"Get off the field, De Grey. Now! Hit the showers and don't come back until I decide if it's worth having a hothead like you on the team. And right now, it's not looking too favorable. Get outta here." Coach threw his hands up and turned to walk toward the far sidelines.

De Grey looked after him, obviously taken aback.

"Coach, come on," De Grey said, starting after him while the rest of the team looked on in surprise. "Coach, I didn't mean anything. Come on. It's not like Matthews is your real son."

Lucas stiffened in surprise. De Grey and his friends had taunted Lucas behind Coach's back, but he never thought De Grey would be stupid enough to say something like that directly to Coach.

Coach whirled and started toward De Grey once more, reaching for De Grey's shoulder pads as Coach Morgan hurried up and stepped between them.

"I'll see that he gets to the locker room, Coach," Morgan said, hooking his hand under De Grey's arm and propelling him away.

The team waited and watched silently as Coach Morgan hauled De Grey toward the field house. They turned back toward Coach expectantly. After several tense moments, he heaved a big sigh and wearily ran his hand down his face.

"Team, it's been quite a workout today," he finally said. "Thank you for your hard work. Let's call it a day but be back in the morning at 7:00 a.m. We'll try to beat some of this heat. Get some water. But remember, drink it slow and easy." After a long pause he waved them off. "Alright, now. Go on."

Lucas' teammates tapped him on his helmet or shoulder pads as they passed him, headed toward the field house. They filed by Coach Holmes, who stood in the middle of the field, his shoulders slumped tiredly, hands on his hips. Lucas came last and stopped.

"Coach . . . I . . ." Lucas began.

He didn't get any further before Coach whirled on him.

"Lucas don't listen to that . . . to that nonsense that De Grey kid spews. Just ignore him," he said as he stepped back and looked at Lucas. "Never doubt but that you *are* a son to me. I want you to know that and hear me say it."

"I know, Coach. I know," Lucas said gently, putting his hand on Coach's shoulder and squeezing it. "Don't worry about De Grey. But I have to admit, I did kinda goad him a bit so . . ."

Lucas looked at Coach with a lopsided grin.

Coach laughed out loud. "Did you now? Well, that's my boy! That sounds like a football player talking," Coach chuckled. "Now, go on. Hit the showers."

Lucas grinned and took off at a jog. He looked back over his shoulder at Coach, who was watching him with a tired smile. Lucas waved and then ran to catch up with Chad and Trevor who had hung back to wait for him.

"You okay?" Trevor asked as Lucas came even with them.

"Oh yeah, I'm fine. I just hate how De Grey gets to Coach. De Grey has a mean streak in him a mile wide."

Both Chad and Trevor nodded their agreement as they reached the field house. "All the better reason to steer clear of the three of them if you ask me," Chad said, opening the door just as De Grey barreled through, crashing into them and giving them each a fierce glare as he pushed his way through.

Lucas exchanged glances with Trevor and Chad, shaking his head.

"Yeah, I think you're right about that."

THE INCIDENT AT PRACTICE had been over a week ago and the first game of the season was tomorrow night. It was the Holmes' tradition to host the team in their home for a meal before the first game. Coach Holmes was grilling burgers and Lucas was helping get things ready. The other coaches and their wives brought everything to go with the burgers, as well as making homemade ice cream and bringing brownies. It was an all-out effort.

After several conferences with the coaches, Joel De Grey's parents, and Joel himself, it had been decided to allow Joel to remain on the team with strict warnings about his conduct. Seeing Joel's parents in Coach's office, Lucas understood better where Joel got his attitude.

Outside of practice nothing had changed. Joel and his friends continued to goad Lucas and make unflattering comments behind the backs of the girls they teased and flirted with. Meg was never told what Joel had said at practice or heard the derogatory comments he made about her and the other girls. She continued to single Joel out for attention whenever she had the chance, just as Joel did with her. Lucas didn't like it or know how to stop it without causing a bigger scene, so he just kept a close eye on both Meg *and* Joel.

MEG LOOKED IN THE mirror and smeared even more bright lipstick on. She pursed her lips together and stood in front of her full-length mirror to check her outfit. She liked it. The cami and tie-up shirt were fine and even though the shorts she'd paired them with were a *little* too short, they weren't that short.

She knew that Joel was coming over—tonight was the night of the annual football season kick-off meal, and she wanted to make sure he noticed her. He'd been paying her a lot of attention lately, saying sweet things, telling her how pretty she was, and always making sure to sit with her at lunch. He always seemed to be watching her.

Meg picked up her phone and smiled, looking at the selfie they'd taken together. Joel had his arm around her, his head touching hers. Meg sighed happily.

Even though Lucas seemed to show up at the most inopportune moments, she enjoyed Joel's attention and wanted more of it. Sure, Joel had been a terror in middle school, but he'd changed. And his good looks didn't hurt either.

"Meg," Lucas knocked on her door and stuck his head in. "We need your help ..."

He stopped mid-sentence. "What is that?!" he asked, pointing with horror at her lips.

She batted her eyes playfully at him. "It's called lipstick."

"I know what it is. But why is there so *much* of it on your lips. It's so ... so ... bright! Your lips are glowing like a neon sign."

"Oh, come on, Lucas!" Meg said with a playful swat. "Don't be so dramatic and such a prude."

"I am not a prude," Lucas said pointedly, "but I am a guy, and I say it needs to come off. Now, before the guys get here!"

"Oh, look at the time. Gotta run help mom," Meg said and dashed out the door before Lucas could stop her.

Lucas stood in the middle of Meg's room with his hands on his hips in frustration. What was supposed to be Meg's bedroom looked more like a tornado ravaged disaster area. He saw Meg's phone where she'd tossed it on her bed. He picked it up. Shaking his head, he looked at the picture of a giddy Meg and a cocky De Grey. He hoped Coach and Patsy could talk some sense into her and especially before the team—and Joel— got here.

MEG EVADED HER MOM'S admonitions to remove the lipstick and change her shorts, while she managed to successfully claim a seat next to Joel. Lucas could only watch and fume. He was afraid for her and knew she was going to end up hurt. After particularly rude comments about some of the girls last week, Lucas and some of his friends had backed De Grey into a corner and told him, in no uncertain terms, to stop. Joel had stopped making comments in front of Lucas but Lucas wasn't naive enough to believe Joel had stopped altogether.

Lucas stayed on the back patio, helping Coach grill the mountain of hamburger patties before he joined the rest of the team filling what seemed like every inch of space in the living room. The burgers were quickly devoured along with the enormous amounts of sides the other coaches and their wives had brought. The sound of conversation, boisterous laughter, and good-natured ribbing filled the living room while Lucas teetered between outstretched legs and bodies, handing out cups of ice cream along with his share of ribbing. Some of the other guys joined in and helped pass platters of brownies.

Patsy was busy in the kitchen, along with the other coaches' wives, scooping ice cream and doing clean-up while the coaches huddled around the nook table, talking strategy. Meg was supposed to be helping too, but she hadn't moved from the corner of the sofa where'd she'd been all evening, sitting close—very close—to Joel. They were talking and whispering in each other's ear. De Grey had his arm behind Meg and was leaning in close to her.

Joel looked up and saw Lucas watching them. He raised his soft drink can and with a sarcastic wink gave a mock salute to Lucas, before turning back to Meg and leaning in even closer. Meg giggled and put her hand on Joel's knee.

Lucas rolled his eyes. He just couldn't watch. He walked back to the kitchen for more ice cream, shaking his head.

"What is it, Lucas?" Patsy asked under her breath as she filled another cup with a mound of ice cream and handed it to Lucas. "Something wrong?"

"No, at least I hope not," Lucas said, setting the filled cup on the plastic tray he was balancing on the corner of the counter. "I just don't like Joel hanging around Meg and how he acts with her. There's just something about him that makes me . . . uncomfortable."

Patsy frowned and laid the ice cream scoop on the counter. Wiping her hands on a dish towel and stepping around some of the other ladies in the kitchen, she walked to the doorway and peered into the crowded family room, trying to get a look at Meg and Joel as people walked between her and where they were sitting.

She turned back to Lucas with concern. "*That's* Joel De Grey . . .?"

Lucas nodded.

Turning back to the family room, Patsy called, "Meg!" a little too loud.

Embarrassed, Meg turned and shot her mom an irritated look.

Patsy motioned Meg to the kitchen. When Meg didn't move, Patsy started toward her. Meg sighed and reluctantly stood. Joel took her hand and held onto it until Meg stepped beyond his reach.

"Yeah, I've heard about him . . ." Patsy said as she came back into the kitchen and resumed her spot scooping ice cream beside Lucas.

"What?" Meg snapped as she entered the kitchen. Seeing Lucas, she stopped short and rolled her eyes.

"Stop it, Lucas," she said between clenched teeth as she stepped to the counter and yanked the full platter of ice cream cups away from him. "Why do you always have to interfere?"

Frowning, Patsy stopped and turned her full attention to Meg. "Put the tray down, Meg and go to your room. Your evening is over." Her tone brooked no argument. "You have nothing to be mad at Lucas about, but you're about to have a lot to answer for if you don't mind me. I will be up after our guests leave and we will talk. Go." Patsy leveled a glare that was not to be defied.

Meg's eyes darted between Lucas and her mother. Furious, she slammed the tray onto the counter with a loud bang, causing Coach Holmes and the other coaches to look up.

Concerned, Coach Holmes looked to Patsy and started to stand, but she forced a smile and waved him off.

"Lucas, I'd appreciate it if you'd go ahead and finish handing out the ice cream. I think it's about time for Coach's annual motivational speech and you certainly don't want to miss that," she said with a teasing grin and small roll of her eyes. "You need to take your place with the team."

Patsy handed the tray to Lucas and with a reassuring smile said. "Don't worry about Meg. I think she has a bad case of teenage-itis."

"Is that what that is?" Lucas said, shaking his head.

Patsy patted his arm. "I'll have a mother-to-daughter talk with her. I don't like the looks of that De Grey either, and I've heard some of the other parents talking about him and…Marty Pierce and Tony Harlow? Does that sound about right?"

Lucas hesitated slightly before nodding then started toward the family room.

"Lucas," Patsy said causing him to pause in the doorway, "you've got a football game to think about. Don't worry about Meg. Okay?"

Lucas nodded, but knew he *would* worry. He'd always worry about Meg.

THE FOOTBALL SEASON WAS off to a great start, and Coach Holmes was extremely happy. The Fort Collins Cougars were 4 and 0 but the biggest game of the season with Fort Collins' archrivals, the Bunkston Badgers, was coming up this weekend. The rivalry between the schools had grown increasingly contentious through the years, with pranks becoming more serious than the fun jabs in previous years. The Bronze Hat trophy was on the line and both teams swore they would be the one to win it this year. Bunkston won last year so Coach Holmes and his Cougars were more determined than ever to win that trophy back.

The local news media was adding to the frenzy, playing up the rivalry, and with the proximity of the two towns, there had been some altercations between players from both teams. With the size of the expected crowd and pregame activities for both schools, the game had been moved from the typical Friday night to Saturday night. The escalating intensity around the game felt more like a state champion-ship than a regular season game.

Coach Holmes and his staff had a difficult job keeping a lid on the players, doing their best to keep the team on an even keel. The players themselves raised the intensity level of Monday's practice, determined to come out on top Saturday night. By the time practice wrapped up, the team was exhausted. It didn't take long for everyone to hit the showers and head home.

Thirty minutes or so after the rowdiness in the locker room had quietened, Coach Holmes stepped out of his office, pulling the door to his office closed after making some notes and doing some paperwork. He was surprised to see Lucas still there, making his way through the locker room picking up discarded towels.

"Lucas?! What are you still doing here? I thought you were long gone by now," Coach said. He walked over to the bench where Lucas had set a large plastic basket filled with wet towels and was leaning tiredly on its handles. "You know Evan will take care of getting everything ready for tomorrow's practice. That's not your job anymore."

Lucas grinned a tired grin. "Oh, I know. I guess old habits die hard. I just thought I'd get a few things done so he wouldn't have as much to do tomorrow. It's a busy week for everyone. I'll be home soon. I've got a big chemistry test tomorrow, so I need to study."

Coach patted Lucas on the shoulder. "We'll wait supper on you. Text when you're headed home so we'll have it ready."

Lucas grinned and nodded as he picked up the basket.

"Oh, and Lucas, lock this door after me," Coach added as he got to the door. "As crazy as things are this week, I don't want you in here alone."

"You worry too much, Coach," Lucas chuckled.

"Humor me, please."

Lucas nodded. "Okay. Okay . . . I'll just put these towels into wash first." He headed toward the laundry room as Coach turned to leave. Lucas heard the door close a few seconds later but as he walked back into the locker room and headed toward the corner to get a broom, he heard the door ease open with a soft click.

"Did you forget something, Coach?" Lucas asked, coming around the end of a row of lockers.

Lucas looked up to see De Grey, Marty, and Tony evidently waiting for him, a steely glint in their eyes. This wasn't good. Something felt very wrong. Lucas backed up a step.

"We thought he'd never leave," Joel said as the three took a step toward Lucas.

"What do you guys want?" Lucas asked, eying the possibility of getting around them.

"We just want to talk to you, Matthews," Joel said, flexing his fingers and releasing them again. "It seems we've had some misunderstandings between us, and we . . . well, we," he said with a glance to either side at Marty and Tony, "we just want to be friends."

Marty and Tony grinned and continued edging toward Lucas.

Afraid of them getting behind him, Lucas backed up again, eying them nervously.

"Well, forgive me, but I don't think that's what you really want, now is it?" Lucas said, trying to sound more confident than he felt.

Joel chuckled, but the smile didn't reach his eyes.

"Well, Matthews, you're not as dumb as you look then."

Joel gave a barely perceptive nod to Marty and Tony. Before Lucas could react, the two grabbed him and slammed him against the wall, pinning him into place, each wrapping an ankle around one of his. It was two against one, and being linemen, they were both much larger and stronger. Lucas struggled, but he couldn't move. He couldn't budge - not even an inch.

Joel stepped up close and looked Lucas in the eye.

"Matthews, you're going to do us a favor. You see," he continued, pacing in front of Lucas, "we had, shall we say, a 'disagreement' with some of the Badgers' linemen." He used air quotes for emphasis. "Things didn't turn out too well for us so you know, we kinda owe them. Actually, we owe them a lot. Which got us to thinking," he glanced between Marty and Tony who grinned and nodded agreement, "that instead of getting back at just those linemen, we could get back at the whole team and win the big game in the process."

Lucas struggled but couldn't move.

Joel shook his head.

"Matthews, be smart. You're outnumbered here. You have no choice, and besides, this is a great plan."

Joel stopped then waited, studying Lucas before going on.

"So this is it. Since you're Coach Holmes *son*," he said with a smirk to Marty and Tony, "you have access to the other team's locker room. Saturday afternoon, you're going to drop one of these in each of their water and Powerade coolers." Joel held up four small plastic baggies with a tiny white pill in each.

Fentanyl.

Lucas' eyes widened in disbelief.

Joel tapped Lucas' cheek with his hand. "Now don't worry, Choir Boy, no real harm will come to them. It will be diluted enough to just slow them up which will give our team the advantage. They'll be lethargic for a few hours and then the effects will wear off with no one being the wiser. It's no big deal. We get our payback, and ultimately, our team, and Coach Holmes of course, gets the W. See? It's a win-win."

Joel waited for Lucas' reaction. When he didn't say anything, Joel lost patience.

"You're doing this, Matthews. You owe us," he spat out.

"I owe you nothing," Lucas said through gritted teeth. "You can forget it. There's no way I'm doing it."

Tony and Marty tightened their grip on Lucas' wrists, causing him to wince.

"I hate to contradict you, Matthews. Truly I do, but you might remember the little incident back in middle school when you interfered with a friendly conversation I was having with Meg Holmes. Do you remember?"

Lucas struggled again, causing Tony and Marty's grip on his wrists to tighten even more.

Joel stepped up to where he was only inches from Lucas. Narrowing his eyes, Joel looked Lucas in the eye and said through clenched teeth, "You meddled in our business, Matthews, and for the little lesson we were compelled to teach you, we were exiled to an 'alternative school' for a month. A whole month," Joel said with a glance to Marty and Tony, "and we haven't forgotten. The time has come for you to pay up for the trouble you caused us."

"You did that to yourself, not me," Lucas said, his breathing short and labored. "I don't owe you—*any* of you—anything. Do to me what you want, but I'm not doing this. I can't make it any plainer."

"Trust me, we *will* do what we want to you, Matthews. You can bet on that, but you're going to do what we say," Joel replied with a sneer. "Or . . . your *sister*, Meg, even though she and I are well, good friends, I'd hate for her to have an unfortunate accident."

At the mention of Meg's name, the color drained from Lucas' face, and he stopped struggling.

Joel grinned. He knew he had him. "You see, we don't take kindly to being bested by the likes of those Badger linemen, so we aim to teach them and their team a lesson. We plan to get even one way or another and that means *you're* helping us—one way or another."

Joel could see Lucas thinking it over, his eyes darting.

"We'll get the pills to you Saturday afternoon. Be here early. Say three o'clock? We found out the Badgers' equipment is being delivered at noon. That will give you plenty of time to drop the pills in before the team arrives. See? Easy but effective."

Lucas couldn't—he wouldn't. But he couldn't let Meg get hurt either. His mind was reeling.

"And Matthews, just to make sure you know we mean business and that we would be *very* unhappy if you were to tell anyone about our arrangement, we'll leave you with this to think about."

Joel pulled back and landed a hard punch straight into Lucas' midsection while Tony and Marty held him tight against the wall.

The air rushed from Lucas' lungs. Before he could get a breath, Joel landed another hard punch. This time Marty and Tony let go of Lucas, and he toppled to the cold concrete floor, clutching his middle and gasping for air.

"Don't forget, Matthews," Joel said, leaning over Lucas and talking into his ear, "Three o'clock Saturday. And not a word to anyone about this or else you *and* your sister will pay dearly."

He gave Lucas one more kick before he, Marty, and Tony laughed and walked out, the locker room door clicking closed behind them.

LUCAS WASN'T SURE HOW long he had laid there, his thoughts spinning, his midsection aching. After several painful attempts, he eventually sat up and took several deep breaths as he tenderly cradled his stomach. The only thing he knew for sure was that he was not going to participate in their plan. Other than that, he had no idea how he was going to protect Meg with her constantly around Joel. Lucas figured Joel had an ulterior motive paying so much attention to Meg. And now, he realized, it may have been for such an opportunity as this.

COACH HOLMES SAT IN his favorite recliner in the family room while Patsy sat on the sofa with her feet propped on a stool. They'd been waiting to hear from Lucas, letting them know he was on his way home. A light dinner was being kept warm in the oven. The TV was on an old western rerun, the sound down low. Coach was trying to get his mind off Saturday night's upcoming game, which was proving difficult to do. Right now, everything revolved around that game.

He heard the kitchen door open and saw Lucas come in. Coach glanced at his watch and frowned, wondering what had kept Lucas so long. It had been almost two hours since he'd left him.

"Lucas?" Coach said as Lucas walked—or more accurately stalked—through the family room, his hand awkwardly clutching his stomach. Coach and Patsy looked at each other, frowning as Lucas went up the stairs without stopping or acknowledging either of them. That wasn't like Lucas.

In just a matter of minutes, they heard Meg yelling and Lucas' raised but firm voice. They looked at each other, standing at the same time and starting toward the stairs. They reached Meg's doorway just as Lucas stormed out and walked quickly to his room. He avoided them but there was a look on his face they'd never seen before.

Exchanging worried looks, Patsy stepped inside Meg's room while Coach went to check on Lucas.

Meg was sitting on the edge of her bed, crying. Patsy walked in slowly and clearing a space in the clutter, sat down beside Meg, putting her arms gently around her.

"What happened, Meg, honey?" Patsy asked softly. "You and Lucas both seem upset."

"Lucas? Lucas? All either of you care about is Lucas!" Meg sobbed.

"Meg, you know that's not true," Patsy said soothingly. "What happened just now?"

Meg gulped a few breaths and then managed to say, "Lucas told me to stay away from Joel De Grey but wouldn't tell me why. It's none of his business who I'm with or who I like! I wish Lucas would just leave me alone!"

Patsy smoothed Meg's silky dark hair and put a hand beneath her chin, forcing Meg to look at her.

"Honey, Lucas isn't one to ask something like that without there being a good reason. I've been hearing some very concerning things for quite some time now about Joel and those boys he hangs out with. I thought you'd stopped spending so much time with him after we talked. You may not like it, but I repeat what I said then—I agree with Lucas and you need to steer clear of Joel De Grey."

"You don't understand!" Meg wailed. "I like Joel. I know he was a bully in middle school, but he's changed. I know he has. He's always nice to me. Lucas just doesn't like him."

"I think you'd have to agree that Lucas seems to like everyone. I've never heard him say anything against anyone, except for Joel and his two friends. Lucas has been around them much more than you have. I'd listen to him."

Meg huffed her disagreement and turned back to her laptop. She wouldn't, couldn't, disagree with her mother outright but then again, neither would she stop hanging out with Joel, at least at school. After all, he'd told her many times about how much he liked her and enjoyed being with her. A guy just wouldn't lie about that.


Lucas stiffened when he heard Coach come in. The bed springs creaked as Coach sat on the edge of the bed across from where Lucas sat at his desk. His midsection still hurting, Lucas sat slumped over, his elbows on the desk. He held his head in his hands, his fingers tangled in his mop of brown hair.

"Son, what is it?" Coach asked, placing a hand softly on Lucas' shoulder.

Lucas flinched at the touch as if he'd been struck. Coach pulled his hand back gently, now more concerned than ever.

"Talk to me, Lucas. Obviously something has happened," he said, his tone firmer.

"No . . . nothing's happened. Everything's fine," Lucas lied. Sniffing, he straightened and ran his fingers through his hair. Turning away, he pulled out a book and opened it. "I've got a chemistry test tomorrow, so I need to study." He bent his head over the book even though Coach could see it was a civics book, not chemistry.

Coach sat for several more minutes, waiting, but Lucas didn't acknowledge him again. Coach finally stood with a sigh, the bed springs creaking again in protest. Coach hesitated briefly at the door with a look back at Lucas before walking into the hall where he met Patsy. They exchanged concerned looks with glances back to both rooms before they walked back downstairs.


LUCAS DID HAVE A chemistry test, but he couldn't focus enough to study. Instead, he ran his fingers through his hair several more times and leaned back in his chair, staring idly at the ceiling as the evening shadows began to creep across the room. He sat up and tugged his wallet out of his pocket. He pulled the picture of Jill out. He studied it, wondering, yet again, where she might be. If they were to meet, would he recognize her? Would *she* recognize him? He wished for the opportunity to find out but she probably lived across the country somewhere or maybe even overseas if her dad was still in the Army. It had been so many years. Still . . .

Lucas slipped the photo back in his wallet and then pulled out the red construction paper leaf from Mr. Andy. What would *he* do in a situation like this? Lucas put his head down on the book laying open in front of him on his desk, the pool of light from his study lamp spilling over and around his head. He thought back, trying to remember some of their many conversations. He could hear Mr. Andy saying, *You've got to look out for yourself, Lucas. But you're going to need friends too.*

Friends . . . Lucas didn't want to get any of the guys on the team involved or even tell Coach — yet. But there *was* somebody he could ask. An idea was beginning to form, and the more he thought about it, it might just solve everything.

L UCAS MADE IT THROUGH Tuesday morning in a blur. He had no idea how he'd done on his chemistry test and didn't remember anything about his other classes. What he did see in vivid detail was Joel De Grey sitting at a table in the cafeteria during lunch, his arm on the back of the chair behind where Meg sat, he and his cronies enjoying a laugh. At least some of Lucas' friends were at the table too.

Meg was playing with fire. And Lucas had to stop it.

Lucas bided his time, talking to some girls who'd stopped to talk to him, but watched and waited until Joel got up to get something else to eat, leaving an empty seat beside Meg. As soon as Joel walked away, Lucas distractedly walked away from the girls and slid into Joel's seat. He put a protective arm on the back of Meg's chair. Meg turned, and upon seeing Lucas, frowned and shot him a hot glare.

"Get away from me!" she hissed as he plastered on a fake smile and started talking to some of the other football players at the table. Amused, Marty and Tony watched the exchange and broke into broad grins when Joel walked up behind Lucas, holding a candy bar in one hand and a soft drink in the other.

"Matthews," he said loudly, "I believe you've got my seat. I was enjoying the company of your lovely *sister*. So if you would excuse us . . ." He moved to push Lucas out of his seat when Mike Simms, Lucas' friend and member of the football team, stood from where he'd been sitting on the other side of Meg.

"Here, De Grey. Keep your shorts on. I'm done. You can sit here."

Meg gave Lucas a triumphant smile, turning to Joel as he sat down.

⁓

Jill Barkley had been to a lot of different schools, her family moving every time her dad was transferred from one Army base to another. The first day at a new school was always the hardest, but lunch on the first day with no one to sit with was especially hard. After registering and having her schedule drawn up that morning, there hadn't been time to meet anyone and certainly no time to make new friends, so Jill was resigned to eating alone and reading a book. She wasn't worried. She knew she'd make friends soon enough.

Jill had just taken a bite of her sandwich when she heard "Matthews" at almost a shout among all the clatter and noise of the cafeteria. It had come from just a few tables over from where she sat. Her heart skipped a beat. Just hearing that name brought back so many wonderful memories. What were the chances this Matthews could be the same Lucas Matthews she'd known in first grade? She'd missed Lucas so much when he and his mom moved. She still thought of him often, wondering where he might be, how he was doing . . .

She froze, her sandwich halfway to her mouth, when her heart suddenly jumped a beat. She looked over, craning her neck, to see the table where the noise had come from and saw the guy—who had evidently done the shouting— ease into a seat beside a girl with long dark hair. The guy sitting on her other side was . . . Jill's breath caught. It was Lucas. It had to be Lucas. She could tell from that mop of golden-brown hair.

She watched him from a distance. He stiffened when the other guy sat down and brushed Lucas' arm away from behind the girl, replacing it with his own. The girl then scooted closer to the other guy as Lucas turned toward them and eyed them closely. When he turned, Jill saw his profile and she knew, without a doubt, it *was* her Lucas. Even with all of the intervening years, she'd recognize him anywhere.

Jill wasn't sure what was going on between Lucas, that girl or that other guy, but she couldn't wait. She had to talk to him. It had been ten years. Quickly tossing the rest of her sack lunch into its bag and gathering her things, she walked to where Lucas sat and stood behind him.

"Your hair is *still* too long," she said, their old, silly greeting nervously rolling from her lips.

Lucas stiffened before he stood and whirled to face her. His eyes lit up and he broke into a huge grin. But just as quickly, his face shuttered and he looked down nervously.

"Lucas! Don't you remember me? It's Jill," she said with an apprehensive smile, glancing at the eager faces at the table watching.

Lucas glanced up but looked down again.

"Yeah, I remember," he mumbled.

The entire table was watching the exchange. The guy with his arm around the dark-haired girl seemed especially interested.

"We just moved to the base. This is my first day here." She tried to go on, but Lucas only looked at the floor.

"Please forgive young Matthews' rudeness," the other guy said, jumping up and extending his hand. "My name is . . ."

"He's a nobody, Jill." Lucas brushed De Grey's hand aside and turned Jill away from the group. Giving her a discreet push, he said under his breath, "Jill, it's good to see you."

His face grew soft, and he gave her a small smile as he looked at her before turning away.

Lucas sat back down, and she heard someone at the table ask as she walked away, "Who was that, Matthews? She's a looker."

"She's a nobody. Just somebody I knew from another lifetime."

Jill heard the group laugh. The talk around the table resumed as she tried to keep walking. She blinked hard, trying to stem the sudden tears at the sting of Lucas' words.

Her sweet Lucas had changed.

LUCAS WANTED TO SCREAM. But more than that, he wanted to run after Jill and grab her into a tight hug and never let her go. After thinking he'd never see her again, it had taken everything within him not to reach out and grab her and shout for joy. But he couldn't—not now—not with Joel De Grey watching.

Why did she have to show up today? This week? Right now, when everything in his life seemed to be dangling on a precipice. He'd always wanted to protect those he loved, but now that was almost beyond his control with Joel's threats and Meg stubbornly clinging to his attention. If Meg only knew what Joel De Grey was really like. If she only knew . . .

But she didn't, and her very life could be on the line because of it.

Lucas sneaked a look over his shoulder as Jill walked out of the cafeteria. He didn't know how, but she'd become even more beautiful. Her shimmering blonde hair hung just past her shoulders and her blue eyes when she'd looked at him were a deeper blue than he remembered. Her oval face was as beautiful and as endearing as in his dreams. *Why?* Why did she have to show up today?

The bell rang and everyone rose to go to their next class. The day was half over, and Saturday was coming. Right now, he needed to focus on Meg's safety. But…Jill was here…she was really here.

W HEN JILL GOT HOME from school that afternoon, she went straight to her room, flouncing down on the bed, tears falling unheeded. The late afternoon sun gave the room a warm glow where it fluttered through the leaves on the large elm tree outside her window. She was mostly unpacked from their recent move, but a few boxes were still scattered around the room. None of that mattered—not right now. She buried her head in the softness of the light blue fabric of her comforter and cried as if her heart were breaking. After all of these years thinking of Lucas, dreaming of finding him one day—never once, in all of those dreams, did she imagine how things had gone today.

*"She's a nobody. Just somebody I knew from another lifetime."*

She heard Lucas' words over and over in her head. His cruel, hurtful words. How could he say that after the friendship they'd shared? True, they'd only been in first grade then and were now seniors in high school, but still, there had been something—a special bond—between them, even back then. Was she the only one who'd felt it? How else could Lucas have blown her off so easily and in front of all of those people?

Jill brushed wayward strands of blonde hair away and reached into the backpack she'd thrown on the bed beside her. She pulled out the old, wrinkled, and torn photo of Lucas from the zippered pocket where she carried it to keep it with her. She looked at the boy in that photo—the kind brown eyes, the bashful smile, and the mop of golden-brown hair. Lucas still looked the same, but he wasn't acting the same now as he had then. She gently stroked the picture with her fingers before fresh tears began to fall. Placing the picture on the nightstand, Jill laid on the bed, wadding a pillow beneath her and cried even harder.

There was a soft knock on her door. Jill paused and reluctantly sat up, dabbing at her eyes.

"Yes?" her voice sounded strangled.

"Honey? Are you okay?" Jill's mom asked worriedly. When Jill didn't answer after several seconds, Jessica added, "Can I come in?"

"Sure, Mom . . . come in," Jill replied, moving to the edge of her bed and running her fingers through her hair.

She swiped her cheeks with the back of her hand as her mom came and sat beside her.

"What's wrong, honey? Rough first day at school? It will get easier. You know it always does. . ."

Before her mom could go on, Jill broke in. "I saw Lucas today."

Jessica sat up, breaking into a broad smile.

"Lucas Matthews? Here? Oh, my goodness! That's wonderful news, but," she added quizzically, "if that's the case, why are you crying? I thought you'd be thrilled to see him again."

Jill sniffed and reached for a tissue on her nightstand.

"*I* was glad to see *him*, but he was less than thrilled to see me. And that's putting it mildly."

Jill relayed the events in the cafeteria, leaving her mother's mouth open in surprise.

"That doesn't sound like the Lucas we knew at all! But if he's here, that means Gloria is here too and . . ."

"No. If you want to find her for my sake because of Lucas, don't bother. He's let me know how he feels. It's just hard to believe how much he's changed."

Jessica stroked Jill's hair absentmindedly as they both sat deep in thought.

"I'll talk to your father, "Jessica finally said, "and see if he can find anything out through the base. There has to be a reason for how Lucas acted. I don't think he could have changed that much. You two were just too close! He may just be having a hard time right now. We don't know. Hang on before you write him off. Okay?" she asked, eying Jill with concern.

Jill nodded hesitantly. "It was just so good to see him . . ." she began, as fresh tears spilled over.

Jill's mom wiped her cheeks gently and then pulled her daughter into a tight embrace.

"Sometimes things are darkest before the dawn. Remember that Sweet Pea," Jessica said with a light kiss to the top of Jill's head.

Jill nodded, taking in the comfort of her mom's familiar soft floral perfume, as her mom held her tight. Jill hoped her mom was right, but it was still going to be hard to know how to act when she saw Lucas again at school. Thinking about it, she resolved she'd have to do the same as he did—ignore him and push him away. That seemed the best—and safest—route for now. She wanted to remember, and believe, Lucas was the same boy as he'd been in first grade, not how he'd acted today.

Lucas nervously paced the floor of the Baker Heights Middle School office Wednesday afternoon. Even though he hadn't been back to this school in three years, everything looked the same. Some of the staff were new but there were still some familiar faces. He clutched the folder tightly in his hand that he had volunteered to bring to Coach Carmichael, who was standing in as defensive coach for Saturday. It could have been emailed but delivering it was a great excuse to talk to Officer Jenkins.

Ever since Monday night, Lucas felt like he had a target on his back and his nerves were on edge. He couldn't continue like this. After remembering Mr. Andy's words of advice about knowing when you needed a friend's help, Lucas had thought of Officer Jenkins. He was a true friend, a police officer, and one Lucas was confident would be more than willing to help.

Lucas hadn't been able to sleep last night. He kept going over the plan in his head, and now he wanted to propose it to Officer Jenkins. Even as focused as his thoughts were, Lucas' mind couldn't help but go back to seeing Jill yesterday. He shook his head. Everything was happening all at once and way too fast. It was all critically important stuff and he had absolutely no control over any of it.

"Lucas Matthews!"

Lucas jumped, nearly dropping the folder.

Officer Jenkins came around the counter, a concerned look on his face.

"Sorry, Lucas. Didn't mean to startle you. You okay?"

Lucas nodded and tried to smile.

"I need to talk to you. I used this as an excuse to come over," Lucas said, flashing the folder in his hand with Coach Carmichael's name on it before glancing nervously around the office.

Officer Jenkins followed Lucas' glance before turning back to see Lucas nervously shuffling his feet. Officer Jenkins put a hand on Lucas' shoulder and said, "Coach Carmichael is off-campus for another thirty minutes. Let's talk in my office. Can I get you some water or a soft drink?"

Lucas didn't realize how dry his mouth was. After Officer Jenkins got him a bottle of water, they both eased into the chairs in front of Officer Jenkins' desk.

Officer Jenkins' office was bare bones. Constantly out on campus, he didn't have much use for an office, but one had been assigned to him for when it was needed, like now. The top of the desk was all but empty except for a phone, a few scattered papers, and a few scattered pens. A credenza behind the desk held some spiral binders and a couple of pictures Lucas assumed were of Officer Jenkins' family.

Lucas took the bottle and tried to screw the top off, but his hands were trembling too badly. Officer Jenkins gently took the bottle from Lucas and opened it before silently handing it back to him.

Officer Jenkins watched Lucas with growing concern, waiting for him to begin.

"Sorry... I guess I'm a mess, aren't I?" Lucas said with a nervous laugh before taking a drink of the water.

"What's going on, Lucas? This must be something serious. I've never seen you act like this, and you coming here tells me you want to talk about it. I'm all ears so whenever you're ready..."

Lucas took another drink of water and heaved a deep breath before looking at Officer Jenkins. Speaking softly, Lucas began, "Well, someone I love has been threatened. Actually, I've been threatened too. They've told me I have to do something for them to keep them from hurting either of us. What they've asked, I can't and won't do, but I have no doubt they'll follow through with their threats. I've thought of a plan but... I need your help."

"Okay, you have my attention. What's your plan and what kind of help do you need? No wait, before any of that, who are we dealing with here? Other students? Adults?"

"Students," Lucas stated but didn't elaborate.

"'I'll need names then. I can't do anything as a law enforcement officer that involves a student without more information."

"I ... uh ... I'd rather not say," Lucas hedged nervously. "Can't we just leave it there?"

"Well no, I'm afraid we can't. It's a serious thing to make threats, whether to a person directly or with intent to harm someone else. Tell me what's going on. You know I'll hold it in the strictest confidence and will do everything within my power to help."

Lucas licked his dry lips and after a long hesitation finally said, "It's Joel De Grey, Marty Pierce, and Tony Harlow. They want me to do something illegal, something that could hurt a lot of people."

Officer Jenkins' eyes widened in surprise.

"Go on."

"I think we can catch them before they have the chance to do anything but still reveal their intent," Lucas said, watching for Officer Jenkins' reaction.

Officer Jenkins nodded slowly. "Okay ... I'm listening. Let's hear your plan."

Lucas went through what he'd been thinking, laying it out step by step, including a clearly defined timeline. It would work. He just knew it would. And then he'd have those bullies off of his back, away from Meg, and away from anyone else they might be threatening.

Officer Jenkins listened thoughtfully, taking notes, until adding the period to the final sentence. He looked at Lucas, who looked exhausted and anxious but equally determined.

"Lucas, this puts you right in the middle of the danger. I can't authorize that. We'll pick these boys up and book them on possession. We've been getting reports of drug dealers making inroads on the high school campuses in the area so this could put a stop to that. Or at least put a big dent in it."

"Sir, it's my sister they've threatened, because of me. If I don't go through with this, they'll find a way to hurt her to get back at me. And then, they'll come after me. I need to make sure she's safe, now and into the future. I truly believe this will work."

Officer Jenkins nodded hesitantly. "Yes, Lucas, I agree. It would work, but it will also put you at serious risk without officers on the inside with you if something should go sideways. This group is always together—never one without the others—so you'd be seriously outnumbered."

"Yes, sir. That's true. But if they really want this done, they won't do anything to me until after it's over, and you'll have them by then. Please, sir. The Holmes have been so good to me, I want to do this to protect Meg and any others in the future they might try to threaten or hurt."

After several minutes in deep thought, Officer Jenkins stood. "Lucas, stay right there." He moved to the other side of the desk and picked up the phone. "Detective Rush, please." After about a ten-minute hushed, but very intense conversation, Officer Jenkins hung up and came back around the desk and sat in the chair beside Lucas.

"I just spoke with Detective Rush in the Drug Enforcement Division at PD. They have been on the trail of Fentanyl drug dealers on Fort Collins school campuses for several months. They think you might have just given them the break they needed. We have tentative approval but there will be a lot of safety measures in place."

Lucas' heart jumped. It was going to happen.

"The first thing is not to say a word of this to Coach Holmes. I know that will be hard, but I also know how much he loves you. I don't think he could keep his feelings from showing after finding out what those boys have already done and are threatening to do. Plus, this involves Fentanyl and you know that what happened with his son, Avery, affected him deeply. That would make it even harder for him to be noncommittal. And if these three get any idea they've been found out, it will shut down the entire plan."

It would be hard to act normal and not tell Coach, but Lucas had managed to make it through a couple of days with only a few more to go. He'd make it work. And what if De Grey, Marty, or Tony did find out somehow? As mean as those three were, Lucas shuddered to think what they could and would do.

Officer Jenkins stood and began nervously pacing the small office as he talked. Lucas watched him, his eyes wide, taking mental notes.

"Go ahead and act as if you're going through with the deal. Continue as you've been at school and be in the field house at three o'clock Saturday, as planned. Accept the drugs from De Grey. The police will already be there and set. At that point they'll be able to catch them in the act when he hands you the Fentanyl. You'll have a phone with a special app that has a mic and it will record everything. It will also enable the police to monitor what's going on in the field house. It's critical that we be able to hear what's happening inside so we can react if needed. Your safety is of paramount importance. But the execution of the operation is also important. This will make a solid, airtight case in court to catch them in the act, with you as witness."

As Lucas listened to the operation's details, Officer Jenkins could almost see the weight lifting from Lucas' shoulders. Yet, another weight descended on him. This was going to be one of the hardest operations Officer Jenkins had ever done, putting a student at such risk. He hoped, in the end, it would be worth it.

When Officer Jenkins finished, Lucas leaned back, the wooden chair popping as he let out a breath he didn't realize he'd been holding.

"Lucas, you'll have Fort Collins' finest right outside the door, out of sight, but nearby. They'll be monitoring everything going on inside and will be there within seconds. The timeline is critical. We don't want those boys in there with you, alone, for any length of time, since we don't know what they might do. I know you've been in tough situations before, but this will be by far the most dangerous. But Lucas, by doing this you could potentially be saving a lot of lives as well as getting drugs, and some dealers, off the street."

Officer Jenkins moved behind his desk, sat down and then stood and began pacing again. He seemed to have as much nervous energy as Lucas.

Lucas leaned over, placed his elbows on his knees, clasping his hands tightly in front of him while silently weighing the enormity of what he was about to do. He wanted to turn time back before Monday night so this nightmare would never have happened. He thought about Meg. Even though she'd been so angry with him the past few weeks, she was still his sister, and he loved her. He couldn't let anything happen to her. And what if De Grey somehow found out how important Jill was to him? Lucas had no doubt De Grey would go after her too.

Lucas knew. He had no choice.

THE NEXT FEW DAYS passed quietly enough. Football practice was rough—not just physically but mentally. De Grey, Marty, and Tony, their eyes glinting when they lined up against the offense, played with fierce intensity. When the play called for Lucas to get the ball, they tackled him hard, a reminder of what was coming, driving their point home again and again.

Lucas and Jill's paths crossed several times at school, but each time she turned away and ignored him. Lucas couldn't blame her. He knew he'd hurt her and that hurt him more than anything. He wished he could pull her aside and tell her what was going on, but he would have to be satisfied until waiting after it was over.

Home wasn't much better. Tension was thick and could be cut with a knife. Coach was so caught up in strategy and planning for the upcoming game, he was oblivious to the anxiousness he was communicating to the rest of the family. Meg refused to speak to Lucas or even look at him over the dinner table or when they saw each other around the house, which had been rare this past week. Patsy watched her family struggling, not understanding all the reasons why, but trying to lend support or play peacemaker when needed.

Lucas dwelt in his own cocoon of fear and dread. He had one more meeting with Officer Jenkins at the middle school on Friday afternoon. He'd get to meet Detective Rush in person and get his final instructions.

Saturday was coming way too fast. And on the other hand, it couldn't come fast enough.

Detective Malcom Rush was a thin, athletic man with salt and pepper hair and a clipped, business-like tone. He wore a nice suit, crisp white shirt, and monotone tie. He looked very official. He was also very intense and to the point. The three of them sat in Officer Jenkins' office late Friday afternoon, discussing the plan and final arrangements. Detective Rush thought it best to meet there, late in the afternoon, when the school and office were closed— fewer prying eyes and ears.

"Lucas, it's pretty straight forward. Go along with everything just as they lined out with you Monday night. Special officers will be staged at all entrances and exits to the field house, in the parking lot, and connecting streets. As soon as the three enter the locker room where you'll be waiting, hit this button on the phone and slip it into your pocket. It will open up a mic to our officers who will have moved in closer once the three are inside. When you say the words, 'Is this it?' that will be their signal to move in. Got it?"

Lucas took the phone and nodded, going through the instructions in his mind again. "Is this it"…that's the signal."

Detective Rush nodded. "You've got it."


Marty Pierce paced in the Baker Heights Middle School's office Friday afternoon. He'd been sent to pick up his little brother's backpack. It was the third time this month it'd been forgotten at school, and Marty was running out of patience. He didn't like playing errand boy. Everyone was already gone for the weekend, and he'd been lucky to catch one last office assistant as she was about to walk out the door. She agreed to fetch his brother's backpack, heading down a long, dark hall. With everyone gone and the school closed, the office was quiet, the hum of a copy machine and an occasional click of a door closing somewhere were the only sounds.

While Marty waited, he walked from picture to picture of past student events or special occasions that hung on the office walls. He smiled at a couple, remembering the fun he'd had participating before Joel recruited him to be involved in ... well, best not to dwell on what he couldn't go back and change. He glanced at his watch and then down the hall but then paused, hearing voices. He edged closer to a door that was cracked open a tiny bit. The voices were hushed but loud enough that Marty was able to catch bits and pieces of what was being said—certain words such as "officers staged," "field house," "is this it," and "signal."

Those phrases and terms sounded like something out of a reality police show when a set up was being planned. But why was something like that being discussed in a middle school? Marty took a fraction of a step closer and his eyes narrowed. He recognized one of the voices—Lucas Matthews.

This couldn't just be a coincidence. Matthews had to be setting them up.

Marty moved quickly away from the door when the assistant finally came back into the office and handed him his brother's backpack. He thanked her and left quickly, hoping not to be seen or heard by the three in the office, should their meeting break up. He especially couldn't let Matthews see him.

He tossed his brother's backpack onto the seat and moved his car across the street so he wouldn't be so noticeable in the empty parking lot. He hunched down behind the steering wheel and waited to see who came out of the office. He had to be sure who'd been in there so he could confirm what he'd heard. He didn't want to give De Grey, or the others, a wrong report. He'd pay dearly for it if he did. There was too much riding on Saturday's 'arrangement' for everything not to be carefully checked.

Thirty-five minutes later, Marty's patience was rewarded when he saw first a tall, slender official-looking guy in a suit leave, followed in a few minutes by Lucas Matthews.

Marty picked up his phone and started texting. De Grey was not going to be happy about this.

$S$ATURDAY MORNING DAWNED BRIGHT and crisp. One of the first true days of fall and the slight chill finally in the air felt good. Lucas wished he could enjoy it, but the afternoon loomed before him like a dark cloud. A smiling Patsy set a heaping plate of pancakes, sausage, and scrambled eggs in front of him. He wasn't the least bit hungry.

"Eat up, Lucas!" she said with a bright smile. "Today is a big day. The Fort Collins Cougars are going to win back that trophy, and then we're going to celebrate with the biggest party you've ever seen!"

Lucas tried to return her smile as he picked up his fork and took a tentative bite of scrambled eggs.

Patsy watched him with a frown as Coach and Meg took seats at the table.

"Ready for today?" Coach asked, as Patsy set a matching heaping plate in front of him.

Lucas swallowed hard. "Yes, sir. I think so."

"He's not very hungry this morning," Patsy commented as she set smaller plates of food in front of her and Meg.

Meg shot a glare at Lucas across the table.

"It's nerves. He'll be fine," Coach said. "I bet the rest of the team is feeling the same way. I don't really like all the buildup that comes with this game. It puts too much pressure on the guys. Well, and the coaches," he said with a wink at Lucas. "It's high school football. Of course, it's exciting and all, but it's not the Super Bowl. Pass the syrup please."

Conversation continued, mainly between Coach and Patsy, as Lucas and Meg remained mostly silent. The parents looked between the two, trying to draw them into the conversation without much success.

Lucas managed to choke down most of his breakfast before asking to be excused.

"Where are you off to?" Patsy asked, eying Lucas over the rim of her coffee cup as she took a sip.

"Oh, just back to my room. Got some prep work to think through," he answered vaguely.

"Thinking? You?" Meg said sarcastically. "You're probably just trying to figure out more ways to make my life miserable."

Lucas winced. He knew she had no idea what was happening today, how much he was trying to protect her, or what Joel De Grey was threatening or even what Joel was *really* like. But still, hearing her say such things hurt.

"Meg!" Coach said sharply.

"I'll be up in my room," Lucas mumbled and headed upstairs.

He could hear sharp words being exchanged as he walked up the stairs. He'd explain to Meg later. He just hoped she'd understand.

Lucas had tried everything he could think of to distract himself. He'd tossed a football in the air while lying on his bed. He'd tried to read but ended up reading the same page over and over. He'd even tried to get ahead with some homework, but nothing held his attention for more than a few minutes. He looked at the clock on his nightstand for the tenth time in the last five minutes and then sighed. He'd be way early but he just couldn't wait any longer. He had to *do* something, not sit here and wait in dread.

He picked up his duffel bag and with a glance around the room, he turned and closed the door behind him.

He stopped at Meg's closed door. He could hear the muffled sound of music coming from the other side. He knocked softly.

"Come in," Meg sang out.

Lucas opened the door and stepped in hesitantly.

"What do *you* want?" Meg asked coldly when she saw him. "Come to give me another lecture about who to hang out with?"

"No, nothing like that," Lucas said softly. "I just wanted to tell you that I love you. That's all."

"Fine. You've told me. Close the door on your way out."

Lucas looked sadly at Meg for several seconds, then nodded and stepped out, closing the door softly.

He stood in the hallway, pinching the bridge of his nose between his fingers. He took a deep breath and walked downstairs. He headed toward the door just as Coach came out of the kitchen.

"Whoa, where are you off to? It's just 1:30. Way too early to head to the field," Coach said, taking a bite of an apple.

"Oh, I know. I just need to be doing something instead of sitting around waiting. Thought I'd get the locker room set up started for Evan," Lucas said, shifting his duffel bag from one hand to the other.

Coach chuckled. "Evan is lucky you're backing him up. It's a rite of passage to handle the logistical stuff, but I'm afraid Evan is more of the gamer type. I appreciate your stepping up and helping out." He gave Lucas a quick pat on the shoulder.

Lucas started to walk on but then he turned back and said softly, "Thank you, sir. Thank you for everything. I'm going to do my best today."

Coach frowned.

"You always do your best, Lucas. I wish the rest of the team were half as conscientious. Is everything alright?"

Lucas ran his sleeve under his nose.

"Everything's fine, sir. Fine. I'd better go."

Lucas walked to the door and opened it, leaving before Coach could say anything more. He had a feeling—a bad feeling—something more was going on than what he knew.

Lucas unlocked the door to the field house and took a deep breath, stepping into the coolness inside. He didn't bother to lock the door since the police were supposed to arrive soon. The familiar smells of ammonia, stale sweat, and liniment met him as he stepped into the darkened interior. He could hear the showers' familiar drip and the popping of the building with the slight wind blowing as he flipped the lights on and dropped his duffel bag in front of his locker.

After setting a bottle of water at each locker, he headed to the uniform room where he picked up the clean jerseys for tonight. He took his time, making his way to each locker, hanging each player's jersey in his assigned locker. Lucas ran his hand over the crimson red material and the bright white satin names and numbers on each. He hung his number 27 jersey with "Matthews" across the back proudly at his own locker. It'd been hard work to make it to varsity, but he loved this team and getting to play for Coach. He just wanted to play football and enjoy his senior year. He wished for the thousandth time he wasn't in the spot where he now found himself. He glanced at his watch again. The minutes were crawling by.

He'd just finished hanging the last jersey when he heard the click of the field house door. He turned, expecting to see Officer Jenkins and Detective Rush but instead Joel, Marty, Tony, and a fourth, older guy Lucas hadn't seen before walked in, stopping at the end of the row of lockers where Lucas stood. The fourth guy was large, muscular, and very intimidating. Lucas swallowed hard.

They were here way too early. The police hadn't arrived, so Lucas had no way to signal for help, which meant there was no back-up. He was on his own.

"Aren't you guys a little early?" Lucas managed, trying to sound as casual as possible.

"So you're Lucas Matthews," the big guy said, ignoring Lucas' question. "I've been hearing a lot about you from my . . . shall we say 'business associates,'" he said, glancing at Joel, Marty, and Tony before taking a step toward Lucas, the others following.

Lucas stole a quick glance at the three as well. For the first time since he'd known them, they looked—nervous. Lucas' blood ran cold and he reflexively took a step backward.

"Come on, Jamison," Joel said between gritted teeth. "Let's get this over with."

Jamison dipped his head slightly, acknowledging Joel's statement before taking another step toward Lucas. "Lucas, it seems you've made it necessary for us to change our plans for today. We heard about your conversation with Officer Jenkins and a police detective. Something about "a signal?" He looked at Marty who nodded solemnly. Jamison took another step toward Lucas.

Lucas couldn't help but flinch. They knew? How?

"I don't know what you're talking about," Lucas tried to say convincingly, looking around for an escape route. He had to get out of there. He couldn't let them stop him.

"Oh, you know exactly what we're talking about," Jamison continued as the four advanced threateningly closer. Lucas backed up another step.

Lockers lined the space with two benches in the middle. The four were blocking his only way out. He had to try something. Lucas knew he was faster than these linemen. If he could get them to let their guard down— just for an instant— he might be able to get past them. He continued to back up, taking a couple of steps, keeping his head down, hands hanging at his side. Even though he tried to remain calm, his ragged breathing sounded loud in his own ears.

The four continued to advance, and Lucas knew it was now or never. He suddenly lunged forward, using every ounce of energy, strength, and speed he owned, bursting through the small gap between Joel and Marty. Caught momentarily by surprise, Marty managed to grab Lucas' sleeve, slowing him down enough to where Tony could tackle him. Lucas fought with everything he had, knocking over benches and struggling wildly. But he was too badly outnumbered. As hard as he thrashed and tried to get loose, Marty and Tony were stronger, and they ended up pinning him solidly to the floor. Joel loomed over him while Jamison knelt beside Lucas' shoulder, shaking his head.

"Matthews, don't make things so hard on yourself. All you had to do was follow our simple plan and all would have been well. But you didn't do it. So now, you've given us no choice," Jamison said, shaking his head with mock sadness.

Jamison pulled out two small clear plastic bags with a small white pill in each. "Since we can't use these on your fine opponents as we'd planned, we had to find another use for them, and we thought of you."

Lucas' eyes went wide and he began struggling even harder.

"Don't. Please. You don't want to do this," Lucas begged. "You're only going to make things worse for all of you. I won't say anything. Just let me go. Please . . . don't . . ."

Joel shook his head. "Matthews, you're such a choir boy. Do you really think we believe you won't tell anyone if we just let you go? I don't think so."

Jamison nodded in agreement, then looking at Lucas said smoothly. "De Grey, hold his head."

Joel grabbed Lucas' head and began forcing his mouth open while Jamison opened one of the plastic bags and picked up the bottle of water Lucas had set at the closest locker.

"Come on, Matthews, for once in your sorry life, make things easy on yourself. It will be quick and painless if you'll just let it," Joel said struggling to open Lucas' mouth.

Jamison carefully took the pill and pushed it between Lucas' lips. He began pouring water from the bottle into Lucas' mouth. Lucas choked and tried to spit the pill out, but Jamison kept pouring the water down his throat, washing the pill down with it. Coughing, Lucas tried to get loose, but Jamison opened the second plastic bag. Joel was trying to force Lucas' lips apart again when car doors were heard slamming outside.

The four looked at each other in alarm.

"I thought you said the police weren't due until later," Jamison growled at Joel.

"They weren't supposed to be," Joel spat out nervously, looking to Marty and Tony, for confirmation. They nodded, still keeping Lucas firmly pinned down.

"Fine. Leave him," Jamison said with a glance at Lucas and stood quickly. "That particular pill is one of our more potent products. It will be enough to do the job. Let's get outta here."

The four sped out the back door, leading to the practice field, but not before Jamison mistakenly dropped the second bag with the pill still inside beside Lucas.

Stunned, it took Lucas several heartbeats to come to himself. He knew he had to do something. He tried to move but his arms and legs weren't cooperating, and his vision was starting to blur. His breath was coming in short, shallow bursts and he felt his chest tightening. He . . . he was already feeling the effects of the Fentanyl. He rolled to one side and tried to stand but collapsed back onto the floor, turning over another bench. He rolled onto his back and stared at the ceiling, wondering how long it would be before . . .

"Lucas!" Officer Jenkins' face appeared on one side of him and Detective Rush on the other as they knelt beside him. Detective Rush picked up the two plastic bags, one empty and one still with the tiny white pill inside. He showed them to Office Jenkins with a direful look.

Officer Jenkins' eyes went wide as he reached into his pocket and pulled something out before reaching for his radio. As if from a distance, Lucas could hear Officer Jenkins calling for an ambulance.

"Stay with me, Lucas. Come on. Stay with me . . ." he heard Officer Jenkins saying over and over. "Come on, Lucas . . . don't let go. Stay with me. Stay . . ."

Lucas felt himself drifting away as he struggled for each wheezing breath. He had to say something before it was too late. "Please tell Coach ... tell Patsy ..." he said weakly. "I'm ... I'm sorry ... I didn't ..."

Lucas couldn't manage any more. He still heard Officer Jenkins talking to him. Lucas was trying, but he felt like he was under water, being pulled further and further down. The blackness was enveloping him. It was the last he remembered.

Coach Holmes was taking one last look at some of the plays he planned to run that night and was putting the folder in his briefcase when his cell phone rang.

"Craig, it's Scott. You and Patsy need to get to the hospital right away." After a slight pause, Officer Jenkins added in a strained voice, "Craig, I'm so sorry . . . it's Lucas."

Coach Holmes reached out to brace himself on the edge of his desk. The room had suddenly started spinning.

"What . . . What do you mean, Scott? What's happened to Lucas?"

Patsy hurried into the room, hearing Coach's voice.

"I'll explain everything when you get here. But please, you need to hurry." The line went dead as Coach turned to Patsy.

"It's Lucas," he said and swallowed hard. "Scott said we need to get to the hospital and to hurry."

Patsy stepped back and put a trembling hand to her throat.

"Craig, no . . . What's happened?" she asked in a weak whisper. She groped for her purse and a sweater as they walked into the family room.

"He said he'd explain everything when we got there. Meg?!" he shouted as he rushed to the closet to get a jacket."

"Meg!"

Meg came sullenly to the top of the stairs.

"Something has happened to Lucas. We're headed to the hospital. Come on. Get a jacket. We've got to hurry," Coach said in a rush.

The color drained from Meg's face as she gasped. "Lucas?"

"Yes! Come on." Coach walked quickly toward the door to the garage.

Meg hadn't moved.

Coach, with Patsy on his heels, turned. "Meg, we can't wait for you. We'll call when we know something."

Coach Holmes brushed Lucas' hair back gently, a tear falling as he looked at Lucas' pale, still form. Lucas looked so helpless, lying in the hospital bed with that big tube taped into his mouth, the ventilator pulsing rhythmically, helping him to breathe. IV lines and monitor wires were everywhere, while a thin sheet and blanket lay lightly over him. He looked so vulnerable, so weak, Coach thought, and Lucas had never looked weak before.

The steady whoosh of the ventilator, the constant beeps and tones of the other monitors, and soft voices from the hallway were the only sounds that broke the heavy silence in the room.

Scott Jenkins and Detective Rush told Coach and Patsy the entire story while they sat anxiously in the emergency waiting room. They explained how Lucas had come to them with a plan, and his ultimate goal of protecting Meg from the harm Joel and his buddies had promised. Lucas had been determined, and it had been an incredibly brave thing to do. Officer Jenkins assured them that everything had been carefully planned. This shouldn't have happened.

Enraged at Lucas being put in such danger, Coach ranted while Officer Jenkins and Detective Rush both stood stoically by, silently agreeing. They understood Coach's anguish and tried to assure him that Lucas' actions and bravery had enabled them to put wheels into motion that would stop a major drug ring's infiltration of the high school campus.

The four who did this had been caught as they ran from the field house. They'd made it as far as the practice field but the police who were in the process of setting up and blocking entrances to the field, caught word over the radio of what had happened and were waiting for them. The four were already booked and in the city jail.

After his initial outburst, Coach apologized to both Officer Jenkins and Detective Rush and now, waited—and prayed—at Lucas' bedside.

Seeing Lucas unconscious and on a breathing ventilator when the doctors finally allowed them into his room, Patsy had broken down into uncontrollable tears. While Coach did his best to console her, the doctor suggested a light sedative and sending her home until something was known—one way or another. Coach agreed and had called some close friends who had picked her up and taken her home a few hours ago.

After she heard what happened and why, Meg refused to come to the hospital and barricaded herself in her room, crying, and refusing to come out.

The news outlets were relaying the word that the game was being postponed and would be rescheduled for a later date. There would be plenty of questions to answer in the days ahead. Coach knew he needed to gather the team and talk to them. They deserved to know the full story of what happened and why, but he couldn't bring himself to leave Lucas. Not until they knew something—one way or the other.

Coach continued at Lucas' bedside overnight and all through the next day, praying and watching, and then praying some more. It had been sixteen hours since everything had happened and there had been no change. Hope was beginning to dim. The doctors said if Lucas didn't show signs of coming around soon, he might not ever. In spite of the use of the opioid-reversing drugs that had helped Lucas start breathing again, some of the Fentanyl had gotten into his system. The side effects were lingering and doctors were monitoring him for 'next steps,' whatever those might be.

Coach took one of Lucas' hands and gripped it tightly, trying to relay as much strength and love as he could through his grasp. He loved Lucas dearly— as much as he'd loved his own flesh and blood son. He hoped Lucas knew that. And if he didn't, that he'd have the chance to tell him.

"Please, Son. We love you, and we need you. Please come back to us. Please wake up," Coach begged through tears.

Officer Jenkins stayed with him throughout the vigil, sitting in the corner of the hospital room, his head bowed, praying too.

IT WAS QUIET. VERY quiet. His breathing, now soft and slow, was the only sound he heard. Then he began to hear soft voices and occasional rumbles of deeper voices. Slowly, very slowly, he managed to open his eyes, but only barely, looking through narrowed slits.

He vaguely remembered what had happened. He'd been struggling to breathe, but he was breathing now— or at least thought he was. Everything was a blur. His eyelids fluttered open a couple more times before closing again as he drifted away.

IT WAS LATE SUNDAY afternoon and until now, Lucas had shown no change and hadn't responded to any stimulus. They'd been able to remove the intubation tube, and Lucas was now breathing on his own. While thankful for it, that had been the only progress. The doctors remained grim-faced when they talked about Lucas' condition.

Coach blinked twice to make sure of what he had just seen. Lucas had opened his eyes, just for a few seconds, but they'd been open before they'd fluttered closed, and he was out again.

"Scott!" Coach said to Officer Jenkins who had fallen asleep in the room's only other guest chair. "Would you get the nurse or doctor please? I think Lucas is trying to wake up."

A few minutes later, Dr. Allison and a nurse hurried in. Coach relayed what he'd seen as they checked Lucas' vitals and the pupils in his eyes, examining the screens of the multitude of machines hooked up to him. After several anxious minutes, Dr. Allison heaved a deep sigh and looked at Coach with a slight smile.

"His vitals do seem stronger, and the brain activity is all good. He may be turning a corner. But he's not out of the woods yet. We'll keep doing what we're doing and monitoring him for more progress." The doctor studied Coach's tired and haggard face.

"Coach Holmes, if you don't mind my saying so, you need a break. You've been here since yesterday, and if Lucas does wake up, you won't want him to see you looking so worried and done in. Why don't you go home and get some rest? We'll contact you if there are any more changes."

Coach looked up at the doctor and shook his head.

"Thanks, Doc, but no. I want to be here *when* Lucas wakes up. I know he will." Coach looked back to Lucas and brushed some hair off Lucas' forehead before placing his hand his shoulder.

As Dr. Allison turned to go, he patted Coach on his shoulder. "He's in my prayers too, Coach."

Coach nodded and smiled distractedly, his eyes on Lucas.

"Come on, Lucas. I know you can do it. Pull from where you keep that inner strength deep inside . . . Please, Lucas. We love you."

Lucas felt himself drifting up from somewhere deep. As he drifted, memories swirled around him. He saw Mr. Andy, laughing and talking about being a firefighter. Mrs. Garrett was there too, smiling and praising him for schoolwork he'd done well. From somewhere else another memory floated by—his first days in a new school and being the target of the class in a dodge ball game. He saw himself being pushed face down in the mud at another new school, more bullies, ruining a new coat his mom had saved for months to buy.

But then he saw Coach, Patsy, and Meg as they all sat around the dinner table, laughing and eating. And then there was Jill, with her golden blonde hair and her deep blue eyes that twinkled when she smiled. She was looking at him and smiling, calling and reaching out to him. But he couldn't reach her or hear what she was saying.

Then he jerked as a powerful memory grabbed him. Four faceless guys were trying to force him to do something . . . something he didn't want to do. He began to struggle as he felt himself rising higher and higher until his eyes popped open to a blinding light. He tried to call out but could only manage a breathy gasp.

"Lucas?"

Lucas blinked. He recognized that voice. He blinked several times, trying to get his eyes to focus.

"Can you hear us, Lucas?" another familiar voice asked.

Lucas moaned and tried to say something, but his mouth and lips were too dry. Seconds later a straw was placed between his lips, and he took a long drink of water.

He heard several low voices, all talking excitedly at once. He was being poked and prodded and a bright light shown, first in one eye and then the other. He tried to raise his hand to brush them away, but something was weighing his hand down, and he couldn't move it. He began to panic, the memory of being forcibly held down seized him, and he struggled against whatever was holding him now.

"Lucas, you're okay. Calm down. We're here with you. Everything's okay, Son. Can you hear me?"

All the voices stopped but this one. He recognized it now. Coach.

"Coach?" Lucas asked hoarsely. "Coach?"

"Yes, Son. I'm here. I'm right here."

Lucas relaxed and took a deep breath. It took a lot of effort, but he eventually forced his eyes open and looked at the circle of faces around him. They were blurry at first but began to come into focus the more he blinked. He only recognized Coach and Officer Jenkins.

"Where . . .?" he asked but couldn't go any further.

"You're in the hospital. And safe. Everything is okay. You just rest, Son. Just rest."

Lucas drifted off to sleep as Coach sat back in his chair. Putting his head in hands, he sobbed with relief, exhaustion, and gratitude. It might take some time, but Lucas was going to be okay.

SUNDAY EVENING COACH CALLED the team together at the field house after the detectives had cleared the area from being a crime scene. He walked reluctantly, his legs, almost of their own accord, taking him to the spot where it had all happened. The benches were sprawled across the floor, the floor still a bit wet. He ran one hand down his face and stood at the edge of the police tape, his shoulders slumped, a hand over his face, the other at his waist. Coach Morgan walked up and put a hand on Coach's shoulder, standing silently with him.

"They almost killed him," Coach Holmes said. He spoke so softly Coach Morgan wasn't sure he'd spoken. "They almost killed him," he said again, his voice rising a degree, shaking his head and wiping his face one more time.

"How could I not have seen what was going on?" Coach said, turning to look at Coach Morgan. "Why didn't I see it?"

"Lucas didn't want you to see it. This was something he wanted to take care of himself. Don't blame yourself for what happened, Craig. None of this is your fault. Except having a hand in raising an amazing young man."

"Thanks, Mike," Coach Holmes said, taking a deep breath.

"How's Lucas, Coach?" Nate Flowers asked as he and the rest of the team silently gathered behind the coaches. They quietly surveyed the police tape in the locker room.

"He's very weak, but he's turned a corner. The doctors think he's going to be okay. It's just going to take some time for him to get back to where he was. Thank you all for coming. I think it's only right that you know what happened, what's going on right now, and what to expect in the future."

The young men and coaches listened somberly as Coach told them the full story. Lucas had a lot of good friends and they were worried about him. Other team members had also had run-ins with Joel and his cohorts, so they weren't surprised something had happened. They were just surprised at the severity of it. For something like this to happen on their team was almost beyond imagining.

"Coach, when can we visit Lucas?" Nate Flowers asked when Coach finished. "We want him to know we're here for him."

Coach smiled. "I know he'll appreciate that, but it'll be a while. He's not up to having visitors right now."

"What's going to happen to Joel and those other guys?" someone else asked.

"The courts will decide that," Officer Jenkins spoke up. "But what they did was attempted murder, so their future doesn't look too bright."

"Uh … if say, we know of some other stuff they were doing, should we … tell someone?" another player asked, noticeably uncomfortable.

Coach and Officer Jenkins looked at each other.

"Yes, absolutely. Anyone who knows anything, come to me privately and let's talk," Officer Jenkins said, looking around at the somber faces.

Several minutes of hushed silence slipped by. Water dripping in the showers and an occasional car passing on the road outside the field house were the only sounds breaking the silence.

Trying to lift the mood a bit, Coach continued. "Some of you may be wondering about the game with Bunkston. The Badgers are grateful for what Lucas prevented from happening, as you can imagine. They said they'd still like to play the game but not until our team feels it's ready and has gotten past this experience—as much as that will be possible. We're in discussions and comparing calendars, but right now, it looks like we'll try to reschedule the game for the week after the final game on the current schedule. I think we'll be ready by then. What do you guys think?" he asked, looking around the room.

"We'll be ready when Lucas is ready. Not a second before," Trevor Singletary said. The rest of the team nodded in agreement.

Pleased, Coach nodded. "Thank you. Thank you, guys. That's great. I know that will mean a lot to Lucas." He paused and took a deep breath. "Alright then. We'll refocus toward next week's game first. And then, let's look forward to getting the Bronze Hat trophy back and winning the game, fair and square!"

O N Tuesday morning Officer Jenkins sat beside Lucas' hospital bed, filling him in on what had been happening since Saturday's incident.

"That fella, Jamison? He's one of the local drug 'bosses' so it was a coup nabbing him. He's clammed up. De Grey, Marty, and Tony are locked up tight. I guess they thought they were untouchable. But when reality hit, they started singing like the proverbial canary," Officer Jenkins said with a small chuckle.

"What did they to tell you that you didn't already know?" Lucas asked, shifting uncomfortably. While most of the tubes and IVs had been removed, a couple still remained along with the tubes for oxygen in Lucas' nose. At times, he thought he was feeling better but then a wave of dizziness or nausea would hit him and he realized he really wasn't feeling as good as he thought. The doctor had said it would take time, but Lucas was impatient.

Officer Jenkins eyed him cautiously. "You, okay?"

Lucas nodded and motioned for him to continue.

"We scored bigger than we thought when we arrested them. As it turns out, those three are the high school contacts for the drug dealing ring we've been trailing the past several months. Their 'bosses,' including Jamison," Officer Jenkins said, using air quotes, "were putting pressure on them to increase their drug sales and had big plans to expand to other campuses. Their goal in going after the Bunkston team, besides winning a football game, was to create more drug users. Those three were really feeling the pressure from their dealers so they were banking everything on coercing you by whatever method it took. They overreached when they went after you."

Officer Jenkins stopped and took a deep breath before going on.

"Marty confessed to overhearing our last planning session and told De Grey about it. And of course, he in turn told Jamison and some of the other drug bosses. They were none too happy their plan had been found out, so they decided to take it out on you."

Lucas' eyes grew even wider.

"Wow. It just goes on and on, doesn't it?"

"Yeah, it's grown far beyond what we ever thought. The charges just keep adding up. And with what they're telling us, we'll be able to seriously curtail, if not end, the drug dealers' hold on the high school. De Grey, Marty, and Tony are still minors, but the district attorney is already in the process of having them tried as adults. After what they tried to do to you, what they'd tried to force you to do, and their drug activities, they're going to be put away for a long, long time. We hadn't been able to catch any of the players in the act, but thanks to you, we were able to catch them. Even though you did go about it the hard way," Officer Jenkins said with a small smile.

Lucas listened and nodded tiredly. Even though it didn't feel like it now, it *had* all been worth it.

"And there's still more," Officer Jenkins said, taking another drink from the bottle of water he'd brought with him.

"Other students are coming forward, talking about their own run-ins with these guys."

Lucas' eyebrows raised in surprise.

"Really?"

Officer Jenkins nodded solemnly.

"Yeah. We've been busy trying to make sure we keep everything documented and record any chain of evidence that's presented in preparation for trial. Speaking of which..." Officer Jenkins paused and took a long look at Lucas.

"Lucas, you do know we're going to need you to testify in court. You'll have to tell it all—what happened in the field house, the attack, the drugs. You know, the full story."

Lucas looked away for several minutes before finally looking back to Officer Jenkins with a resigned look. He nodded, his hair rustling against the pillow.

"Yeah, I kinda figured that would be the case," Lucas said softly. "But that doesn't mean I'm looking forward to it."

"That's understandable," Officer Jenkins assured him. "But know this—there's nothing he or any of his cronies can do to you, Meg or anyone else you care about. Not anymore. They're going to be lucky to ever see the light of day again."

"How can anybody be so dumb as to think they could get away with all that they did?" Lucas asked, shaking his head. "It makes no sense."

"I'd have to agree with you," Officer Jenkins acknowledged as he stood. His phone buzzed and he pulled it from his pocket, glancing quickly at the screen. "Well, as I said we're pretty busy right now, but I wanted to come by and check on you and let you know what was going on." He paused and seemed to consider what he wanted to say before going on. "Lucas, you're tougher than almost anybody I've ever known, adult or otherwise. It took real guts to do what you did, and I truly admire you for it. But please, let's not do it again. Okay?"

Lucas grinned, the first genuine smile he'd managed since everything had happened.

"Thanks, Officer Jenkins, and I totally agree. Let's not do this again," Lucas said as they shook hands.

"Do what again?" Patsy asked as she came into the room. "Scott, you'd better not be recruiting Lucas for anything else. I will have to absolutely forbid it," she said with a teasing smile but firm tone.

"No, ma'am. I wouldn't dare dream of it. I'll see you both later."

Patsy smiled and took the chair Officer Jenkins had just vacated. She'd been spending the days with Lucas while Coach spent the evenings after school. They'd tried to get Meg to visit Lucas, but she refused. It nearly broke Patsy's heart every time she came to Lucas' hospital room, and he looked eagerly behind her, hoping to see Meg.

"Hey," he said, his face wan and his smile still tired.

"Hey, yourself. Sleep well?"

Lucas nodded slightly and looked around the room.

"Meg not come again today?"

Patsy shook her head sadly.

"I'm sorry, Lucas," Patsy said, stroking the side of his cheek with the back of her hand. "We've tried to talk to her, but she blames herself for putting you here. She's too embarrassed and says she just can't face you."

Lucas frowned and looked away. "She didn't put me here. I did that myself. But I had to keep them from hurting her. Joel threatened . . ." Lucas turned away and couldn't go on.

"Don't dwell on it or even think about it. We're just thankful you're alive and getting better. Meg will soon come to realize that she's one very lucky girl to have a big brother who loves her as much as you do."

Their conversation was interrupted by Dr. Allison coming into the room with a wide smile, bringing scattered noises from the hall in with him. He walked to the foot of the bed where the rolling table sat with most of Lucas' breakfast still on it.

"Good morning, Lucas, Patsy," he said with a nod to each of them before rushing on to say, "I have good news, Lucas. How would you like to go home?"

Lucas scooted up in the bed, his eyes brightening.

"Really? I can go home?"

"From what I'm seeing in your last test results, you're well on the way back to being a hundred percent. I think being at home will help you get there faster than being in the hospital. You'll spend one more night here so we can monitor you just a bit longer, but then you'll go home in the morning. Sound good?"

"Yes, sir! That sounds great," Lucas said with renewed energy. "But if I go home in the morning, what does that mean we'll be having for lunch? The food here isn't exactly the best." He looked to Patsy. "So, I'm planning on being *really* hungry."

Patsy broke into a bright smile and laughed.

"Whatever you want, Lucas. You just name it."

COACH HELD THE DOOR into the kitchen open as Patsy held Lucas under one arm and Coach supported the other, walking slowly with him to the family room.

"Guys, I think I can manage getting from the car to the family room without all this fuss," Lucas tried to joke. But the paleness of his face and his trembling hands told a different story.

They eased him down onto the seat in the sectional he'd claimed as his own from his first day with them. His head fell back onto the sofa and he released a deep breath.

"It sure is good to be home," he said, looking up at Coach and Patsy with a shaky smile.

"Well, I'm going to start lunch," Patsy said. "Homemade pizza and chocolate cake coming right up."

Patsy had started to the kitchen and Coach had started toward his office when they all three looked up to see Meg standing at the bottom of the stairs, looking at Lucas hesitantly.

"Meg," Lucas said softly, waiting for her to say something as he sat up straighter on the sofa.

"Lucas, I'm so sorr. . ." Meg didn't finish but ran and jumped onto the sofa beside Lucas, throwing her arms around him, crying.

Lucas hugged her as tightly as he was able, patting her back. "It's okay. Don't cry."

"Don't be so nice to me!" Meg said, raising up and swiping angrily at the tears. "I was horrible to you, Lucas."

"Meg, please. Really. Everything's okay," Lucas said. "I'm here. They're not. End of story."

"No. It's not okay and it's not the end of the story," Meg said, looking Lucas in the eye and taking one of his hands in her own, holding it tightly.

"Lucas, I have been so foolish. You were right about Joel and those other two. It's embarrassing to admit, especially in light of what you've been through, but I was carried away and flattered by the attention Joel gave me. I thought he was so cute and so charming, and he said all the right things, and I . . . believed him." Meg looked down and sighed sadly.

Lucas watched Meg and waited for her to continue, feeling what she said next would be important and probably what she'd been working through for herself the past few days.

"I've learned a hard lesson—a very hard life lesson," she finally said, reluctantly raising her eyes to meet Lucas' concerned gaze. "I've learned that you can't judge a book by its cover. Some books, like Joel, look great on the outside but they're ugly and mean on the inside. And then there are other books," she stopped and with a small smile said, "that look just as good on the outside as they are good on the inside, like you, Lucas. You are the best big brother any girl could be lucky enough to have. I'm sorry my blindness put you through so much when you were looking out for me. I was just too stubborn and selfish to realize it. I love you, Lucas. Can you ever forgive me?"

Lucas was physically exhausted, but he mustered a tired smile, looking Meg directly in the eye. "Of course. I love you, Meg, and always will. Nothing will ever change that. But promise me you'll always know how very much you are worth and how much you are loved. Never, ever let someone like Joel De Grey dictate your value or how you feel about yourself."

Meg nodded solemnly as a tear found its way down her cheek. "I promise, Lucas. I promise."

Lucas reached up and brushed the tear away with his thumb. He broke into a teasing grin.

"I do have a question though . . . about that analogy you used?"

Meg looked at him quizzically. "A question?"

"Yeah, so . . . are you saying you think I'm good-looking?" Lucas teased, unable to resist a small chuckle.

Meg laughed and shook her head, smiling. "Oh my. Did I say that? What I meant to say was that *my friends* all say you're good-looking."

"Oh," Lucas said, his face turning red, "I was just kidding."

"But I'm not," Meg replied with a laugh. "They really do say that! Oh, and there's another thing . . ."

"There's more?" Lucas asked. "I can't keep up with it all."

Meg frowned playfully before continuing. "Yes, there's more, and you'll be glad. I've decided to be the best sister you'd ever hope to have. No more giving you a hard time. No more arguing with you. No more . . ."

"Wait, hold up," Lucas said, laughing lightly. "How am I supposed to recognize you then?"

Meg gave him a light swat and they both laughed.

"Meg, honey," Coach said, "Lucas is still a bit weak so let's let him rest, okay?"

Meg's bottom lip trembled at the reminder.

"Lucas, really—I love you. And I am so sorry, so truly sorry."

"I love you too, Meg," Lucas said, his voice hoarse. "I guess this means I'll still have to put up with you."

"Oh yes, you absolutely do have to put up with me. No way you're getting out of it." Meg hugged him again before sitting up and wiping at her eyes with the back of her hand. "Okay, now," she sniffed, "how about we watch a movie so you can rest?"

"Sounds good. What's it gonna be?" Lucas asked, pointing the remote Coach handed him at the TV.

"I don't care. I just want to be here with you."

Lucas smiled and pulled up a mutual favorite. Meg looped her arm through his and put her head on his shoulder and pulled him close as Patsy spread a throw over both of them.

Coach and Patsy watched and listened and then shared a happy smile. Their family was together again and complete.

Early Saturday evening, after several days of steadily regaining his strength, Lucas approached Coach. "Would you drive me somewhere? There's someone I need to talk to."

"Anybody I know?"

"No, sir. At least not yet. But I hope you will soon."

As Coach drove, Lucas silently studied the text on his phone that Officer Jenkins had sent with the address Lucas had asked him to find. When Coach pulled up in front of a nice, modest home near the Army base, Lucas' heart sped up.

"I'm not sure how long I'll be. Maybe not long," Lucas said softly.

"Take as much time as you need, Son. I'll be here."

Coach watched as Lucas got out of the car, awkwardly maneuvering the cane the doctor had recommended until he was steadier on his feet. He slowly made it up the short walk and carefully stepped up onto the porch. As Coach watched, Lucas raised his hand to knock but before he could, the door flew open and a girl with long blonde hair launched herself into Lucas' arms, nearly knocking him over. Coach smiled and looked down to read the book he'd brought along, just in case.

"Lucas!" Jill kept saying over and over as she hugged him tightly. "Are you okay? I heard about everything at school and couldn't believe it. Are you okay? I heard you were you hurt."

Lucas wobbled a bit. Jill looked down and saw the cane. "Oh Lucas, I'm so sorry. Please let's sit over here," she said, motioning to the two wicker chairs and the love-seat on the front porch.

Smiling, she took his hand as they sat down together on the love-seat.

"I think I have to touch you…just to make sure you're real," Jill said, squeezing Lucas' hand.

Lucas looked at Jill hesitantly. She was even more beautiful than he remembered from the quick glance he'd gotten in the cafeteria. Her blonde hair hung past her shoulders, a few strands lifting in the evening breeze. Her deep blue eyes were shining and watching him expectantly. Her cheeks were rosy pink and her smile made his heart flip.

"Jill," Lucas began nervously looking from her hand holding his to her eyes, "I owe you an apology for what I said and did the other day." He looked deeply into her eyes.

"There was a lot going on right then, and I didn't want those guys to know that you and I are well, you know … friends. It took everything I had not to whoop with joy and grab you up into a big hug right on the spot. If I had, I'm not sure I could have ever let go." Lucas tried to chuckle but could only grin self-consciously.

Jill smiled a radiant smile and put her other hand on top of Lucas'.

"You owe me no apology, Lucas. After hearing what all had happened and knowing you like I thought I remembered you, I realized something had to have been going on. It only made me …"

Jill paused for several seconds. "Almost made you what, Jill?" Lucas asked shyly. He waited patiently before she finally looked up at him again.

"It only made me love you more," she said, looking him straight in the eye and heaving a big sigh. "Oh, Lucas! I was so upset when you and your mom moved. I missed you so much. We looked for you—we all looked for you—after you moved. My parents searched, talked to people, checked with other Army bases. They did everything they possibly could. It was like you and your mom had just disappeared. I thought I was never going to see you again. And then seeing you the other day after so long, Lucas, I just—"

Lucas nodded somberly and squeezed her hand. "My mom and I, we moved around—a lot. She was never the same after my dad died. She never could keep a job, so we were always on the move. Money was scarce, if existent at all. When she died, I went into foster care and bounced from house to house for years. That is, until I met the Holmes four years ago. They changed my life and gave me a real home with love and support."

At that moment, the front door flung open, and Jill's mom and dad spilled onto the porch in a flurry of hugs and exclamations at seeing Lucas again. Lucas found when he started smiling, he couldn't stop. Seeing them again brought back so many wonderful memories. He'd missed them even more than he'd realized.

After talking with Lucas briefly, and after he promised to come back for dinner when he was fully back on his feet, Dan and Jessica exchanged knowing grins. They clasped Lucas in one more hug and a firm handshake before they went back inside, leaving Lucas and Jill alone.

They settled back onto the love-seat as a comfortable silence fell between them. Jill smiled and put her hand gently to Lucas' cheek.

"Lucas, you haven't changed a bit. You're still the sweet, kind boy I met in first grade. And whose hair is still too long," she said playfully.

Lucas threaded his fingers through hers, saying, "Yeah and yours is still too blonde."

They looked deeply into each other's eyes for several long seconds before they both leaned forward. Their lips touched tentatively at first and then more firmly. Lucas felt like he'd finally found a missing piece of himself.

Reluctantly breaking the kiss, Jill leaned back and looked at Lucas with a frown.

"I shouldn't be so forward," she said. "You've probably got lots of girlfriends."

"Well, no, actually I don't. I just have one...as of right now," Lucas said, smiling.

L UCAS HAD MISSED TWO weeks of school before he felt strong enough to attend classes again. He'd gone to football practice a couple of times as a sidelines observer, acting as an assistant to Coach, but hadn't gone back into the field house—at least not yet.

When he began light practices with the team, he hesitated the first time he had to walk in the field house door and then into the locker room. It was hard seeing where everything had happened, but the team, seeming to know ahead of time that would be the case, surprised him with an impromptu party, playing loud music and keeping him rowdily occupied the entire time they dressed out for practice.

It felt good to be back. No—it felt great to be back. Those guys who had tormented him for years were now permanently out of the picture. And Jill . . . Jill was back *in* the picture. It just didn't get any better.

The big rivalry game came and went without much fanfare. Bunkston won the trophy again. And while the game had been intense, it had also been friendly. Before the game, the Bunkston High School principal and head football coach presented Lucas with a plaque of appreciation in front of both teams. During the short speeches, Lucas shuffled his feet nervously and looked down, uncomfortable at the attention for something that had been so difficult to get through.

After the football season ended, Lucas resumed his part-time job at Auto Works, the local tire and oil change service store. He worked back in the service bay installing or changing tires and doing oil changes. It was dirty work—hot in the summer and cold in the winter. It kept him busy almost every day after school, but it paid surprisingly well. And that was the most important thing, since he was setting aside as much money as possible to attend the fire academy.

Jill and Meg became close friends and spent a lot of time together shopping and doing "girl stuff" as they called it. Lucas was thrilled that the two most important girls in his life had become such good friends. He didn't mind, too much, that they both tended to dote on him either.

Thomas Bender, a prosecutor with the District Attorney's office, contacted Coach and Patsy, and then Lucas in late March, letting them know the trial for Joel De Grey, Marty, and Tony was on the court docket for May. The three defendants had decided to be tried together, which was speeding up the process. Mr. Bender asked Lucas to reserve several dates to make sure he would be available to be in court to testify. Mr. Bender had also asked to schedule some time with Lucas prior to the trial to go over his testimony. Lucas dreaded the whole affair. He didn't want to relive those terrible moments or see those three again, but he also knew he'd do what was needed.

The Christmas holidays and the winter flew by. And as spring and graduation arrived, the students didn't have time to realize how quickly the school year was coming to an end.

Talk of college applications was also in the air and served as a great distraction. Lucas listened to his friends talking about where they were applying, their test scores, and what campuses were the most fun. He hadn't planned to attend college—at least not right away. His plans were to attend the first available firefighter training academy at District Five after May's graduation. Lucas had carefully made his plans and was working his plan. He was ready.

One afternoon in early April, Lucas excitedly sat down with the goal of completing and submitting his application to the fire academy. It was time. He pulled up the now familiar website and downloaded the application. He completed it and moved on to the payment section. He examined the numbers and re-examined the numbers again.

They'd changed, increasing by a lot since he'd last looked at the site just a couple of weeks ago.

Lucas sat back in his chair, staring at his laptop screen and ran his fingers through his hair. No matter how he figured it, he didn't have enough money. He had enough to pay for the firefighter academy but not for the paramedic training. The courses had to be completed within a few months of each other for both to count toward applying with any fire department. He sighed in frustration. He was close—so close. With the limited time he had available, he could ask for more hours at Auto Works but even with that, it wouldn't be enough to make up the difference. He might have to wait until the next fire academy class, but he didn't want to wait to make his firefighting dream a reality. There had to be a way to work this out. There just had to be.

T<sup></sup>HE SCHOOL YEAR WAS entering its final phase and senior activities were about to begin in earnest as the trial arrived. Lucas looked up at the courthouse as he walked in that morning. Even though Lucas had given a recorded deposition, he still had to testify in person. He was ready. And now, the day had come. He just wanted it to be over so he wouldn't have to keep reliving those bad experiences.

Everyone had been surprised at how quickly things had moved when the trial date for Joel, Marty, and Tony had been set for the first week of May, right before graduation. While this trial was for Joel, Marty, and Tony, Jamison, the fourth person in the field house that afternoon, was being tried separately. There were several more charges against him as leader of one of the local drug gangs.

Mr. Bender had talked to Lucas at length about his testimony and cautioned him about how the defense attorney might try to twist his testimony or try to trip him up under cross examination. At the end of their conversation, Mr. Bender looked Lucas in the eye and smiled.

"Lucas, my boy," he'd said, tucking his fingers beneath his suspenders as he paced in the conference room where they'd been meeting the past week, "you're a prosecutor's dream. You're honest, you're humble and you're not vengeful. No, you're going to do great."

Mr. Bender took a seat in the conference chair at the head of the table. "Just tell them what happened like you've told it to me—straight forward with no embellishments and it will be over before you know it."

Lucas pulled at the collar of his shirt. He wasn't accustomed to wearing a suit and tie. He felt like he was choking. But this was what Mr. Bender had told him to wear when testifying in court. Lucas leaned forward, putting his elbows on his knees and his head in his hands. Coach, sitting across the table, checked his watch with a glance over at Officer Jenkins who was leaning against the wall, looking at his phone.

The small room in the courthouse where they waited was warm and stuffy. It held a small conference table and four wooden chairs. The walls were bare except for one which held a small window. Mr. Bender had told them to be there an hour ago, but then there had been a delay in the courtroom, so things were behind schedule. Dan and Jessica along with Jill, Patsy, and Meg were already in the courtroom but had given Lucas hugs and smiles of reassurance before they'd parted. They were saving seats for Coach and Officer Jenkins.

"How ya doing, Lucas?" Officer Jenkins asked, glancing up and catching Lucas' eye as Lucas straightened in his chair. Walking the few steps possible in the room, Officer Jenkins came to a stop by Lucas and sat on the edge of the wooden table, facing him.

"Oh, I'm fine. Just ready to get this over with," Lucas said, letting out a deep breath. He looked up at Officer Jenkins who was studying him intently, his kind face lined with concern.

"Officer Jenkins," Lucas said in a hushed voice, "I don't know how I didn't know until I heard about your testimony yesterday, about what you did in the field house that afternoon."

"Yeah? What did you hear?" Officer Jenkins asked with a small smile.

Lucas cleared his throat. "Well, I heard that you gave me some kind of opioid reversal drug that helped me start breathing again before the paramedics and ambulance got there."

Officer Jenkins nodded. "Yes, I did. With the drug situation at the schools escalating in the past months, it's standard now for resource officers to carry a reversal drug that can be administered in an emergency. Every second is critical in a situation like yours. I'm sure glad I had it that day."

"I am too," Coach Holmes interjected with a smile Lucas' direction.

"Well, and me too. It seems you keep saving my life, one way or another," Lucas added, returning a small smile. "I'll never be able to thank you enough for . . . well, for everything."

"No thanks necessary, Lucas. You being the fine young man you are, that's thanks enough for me. You're the kind of student that makes my job worthwhile. I'm proud of you."

"I appreciate that, sir. But you might want to wait to say that until you see how things go today. I could blow the entire case if I don't get this right," Lucas nervously chuckled.

Officer Jenkins just laughed and shook his head. "I'm not worried in the least."

Lucas grinned slightly but anxiously began drumming his fingers on his knees.

"How much longer do you think it's going to be?" Lucas asked with a look toward Coach and then Officer Jenkins.

"There's no way to know, but—" Officer Jenkins began before the door opened suddenly and the bailiff stepped in.

"Lucas Matthews?"

Lucas stood, pulling his suit jacket down and straightening the tie Coach had loaned him. "Yes, sir."

"They're ready for you. Follow me."

The bailiff turned and started down the hallway that led to the courtroom. Lucas began to follow, but Coach stopped him and gave him a quick hug as Officer Jenkins clapped him on the back.

"We'll see you inside," Coach said with a confident smile. "You're gonna do great."

Lucas took a deep breath and followed the bailiff to a closed wooden door. The bailiff waited for a signal before opening the door and stepping into the courtroom with Lucas following a step or two behind. The first thing Lucas felt more than he saw was the large number of people in the room.

The courtroom was enormous with a vaulted ceiling and recessed florescent lighting that brightened the ceiling and the room below. The judge, imposing in his black robe, frowned down on Lucas from his elevated seat behind a large desk of golden wood polished to a high shine. As Lucas followed the bailiff to the witness stand, he turned to face the room, and saw Joel, Marty, and Tony for the first time. They were sitting at wooden tables the same color as the judge's desk. Each was dressed in a suit and tie, just as he was, an attorney beside each of them.

Mr. Bender and two other attorneys Lucas had met previously were seated across the aisle at a table matching those of the defendants. Directly behind the tables and their occupants was a short wall that ran the length of the courtroom. Directly behind it, on the front row, sat Dan and Jessica, Jill, and Patsy and Meg with Coach and Officer Jenkins sliding into seats beside them. A large crowd of spectators filled the other seats. Even though Lucas knew he was the victim and had nothing to fear, this was intimidating.

Lucas tried to avoid looking at the three defendants, but his gaze couldn't help drifting toward them. They looked so different from the cocky cruel bullies who had threatened and tormented him for so many years. They seemed smaller somehow but when Lucas looked their way, the three stared at him with defiant glares.

Lucas' attention was brought back to Mr. Bender as he rose and moved to a small podium on which he placed several pages of notes. The courtroom stilled. Not a sound was heard except for Lucas taking a shaky breath as everyone waited for Mr. Bender to begin. He had just started his first question when one of the large double doors at the back of the courtroom opened with what would have otherwise been a quiet swish if the room hadn't already been so quiet. Trevor Singletary entered first followed by Nate Flowers, then Chad Bloom, then Cody Peters, and on and on until every member of the Fort Collins Cougars football team had entered and took places to stand along the courtroom's back wall.

Lucas sat a little taller as his teammates nodded subtly to him or simply stood resolutely shoulder to shoulder with solemn looks of determination. After turning and watching their former teammates enter, Joel, Marty, and Tony turned back to face the front, their air of self-important confidence seeming to deflate.

Mr. Bender turned around, facing Lucas, doing his best to stifle a smile as the judge pinned him with a questioning look.

"Mr. Bender, is this bit of drama something you cooked up for the court today?" the judge asked, pulling his glasses off and studying Mr. Bender pointedly.

"No, Your Honor. I had no idea these gentlemen were planning to come today."

"We object, Your Honor," Mr. Jacobs, the defense attorney said, jumping up from his seat. "This is nothing but a show to distract the jury. We ask that they be removed from the court," he huffed as the other two defense attorneys nodded vigorously in agreement.

Lucas looked between the battling attorneys and caught Coach's eye. Coach was doing his best to hide a grin and gave Lucas a discreet wink.

The judge twirled his glasses for several seconds, seemingly deep in thought before slipping them back on. He picked up some papers in front of him, tapping them on his desk to straighten them before saying, "Your objection is overruled, Mr. Jacobs. These young men have a vested interest in these proceedings as they know the participants in this trial. They're allowed to stay. Mr. Bender, please proceed."

"But . . ." Mr. Jacobs tried to protest again.

"Sit down, Mr. Jacobs," the judge said firmly, now with a glare, then turned to Mr. Bender. "Proceed, Counselor."

Frustrated, the defense attorney dropped into his chair as Mr. Bender nodded with a confident smile.

"My pleasure, Your Honor." Turning to Lucas, Mr. Bender began, "Mr. Matthews, if you would please relay to the court what happened this past fall on Monday, October 12."

Lucas' testimony was succinct, factual, and to the point. Even though the team had heard the basic facts from Coach, this was the first time they'd heard the details directly from Lucas. Some shifted angrily as Lucas related the details of both incidents, the threats made by Joel, Marty, and Tony and what had ultimately happened the afternoon they'd forced the Fentanyl down his throat, almost killing him. Lucas had gone over what happened several times with Mr. Bender but telling it in court was more difficult than what he'd thought it would be. He choked up a couple of times but managed to get through it.

At the conclusion of Mr. Bender's questioning, Lucas shifted nervously in the witness chair and took a drink from the bottle of water left for him on the stand, waiting apprehensively for the defense attorney's turn to ask questions.

When Mr. Jacobs stepped to the podium and began, he was pointed and fast paced, haughtily trying to trip Lucas up, asking the same questions quickly and several different ways. He took facts Lucas had already testified as happening and tried to twist them.

Mr. Bender objected at the line and manner of questioning several times, accusing Mr. Jacobs of badgering the witness. Jill and her parents, Coach, Patsy, and Officer Jenkins squirmed angrily in their chairs as the defense attorney attacked Lucas repeatedly, trying to shake his testimony. When Mr. Jacobs started on Lucas' background and being in foster care, the judge quickly stopped that line of questioning as irrelevant after a strenuous objection from Mr. Bender. Lucas' testimony continued over the next hour. The judge sustained several more objections from Mr. Bender but overruled others, leaving Lucas emotionally and physically exhausted when it was finally over.

When the judge said the court would be in recess until the next Monday and told Lucas he could step down,

Lucas was more than ready. After the judge and jury left, and Lucas started to step off the witness stand, Mr. Bender quickly approached, extending his hand to Lucas.

"Well done, Lucas. Well done. Jacobs is a snake on defense and you parried with him well. If anything, you strengthened your testimony. You shouldn't have to come back, but we will let you know. Now, go on. I think your family and your teammates would like to congratulate you. And son, I'm just sorry for what you went through. It looks like those three are going to be put away for a long, long time."

Lucas nodded and wearily shook Mr. Bender's hand.

"Thank you, Mr. Bender. And no offense, but I hope I don't hear from you again."

Mr. Bender laughed and slapped Lucas on the back. "No offense taken, Lucas. I totally understand. Now go on."

Lucas took a few steps and into Patsy's open arms as she hugged him tightly while Coach shook Lucas' hand before pulling him into a hug himself. A pale Meg hugged him, followed by Officer Jenkins pumping Lucas' hand energetically. Lucas' teammates then surrounded him, patting him on the shoulder, tousling his hair or giving him a good-natured shove. Jill and her parents waited to the side, watching and smiling. After Lucas had shaken the hand of every teammate, thanking them for coming and for their support, he made his way over to them. Dan shook his hand and Jessica gave him a warm hug. When Lucas turned to Jill, he pulled her to him, clenching her to him firmly.

"I'm so glad you were here," he said softly into her ear.

"No where else I'd be than with you, Lucas."

As the doors to the courtroom opened and the group left together, Lucas clasping Jill's hand firmly in his own, he felt like years' worth of a heavy load had finally been lifted.

SENIOR WEEK ROLLED AROUND. Since the seniors had completed their finals the week before, this week was for ceremonies and celebrations. Before baccalaureate and commencement took place, one of Fort Collins High's key time-honored senior celebrations was Senior Sound Off. It was an entire afternoon centered around the senior class. Incoming freshmen were invited to the campus for the afternoon to see and experience a taste of what life was like at the senior high level. It was a fun and festive afternoon, but it also turned nostalgic when everyone realized these seniors were moving on.

Everyone filled the auditorium after lunch where the orchestra performed a couple of songs, followed by the choir's performance of two or three numbers. The two groups then performed one selection together. There were some speeches and awards presented, both serious and fun, and recognitions were made.

For the most anticipated event of the afternoon, the sophomore and junior classes had voted and selected the five seniors they would most like to hear from. No one knew who the final top five were except for the principal, who tallied the votes and contacted those selected. It was a huge honor, and speculation ran rampant in the weeks leading up to the Senior Sound Off. The wide range of possible questions submitted added another element of surprise.

The packed auditorium was electric with anticipation as the principal moved to the podium. The noise died down almost immediately.

"Good afternoon, everyone and welcome to Senior Sound Off," Principal Harrison began. "Without any further ado, let me introduce to you the five seniors *you* have selected to hear from this year."

The front of the stage was bathed in bright light where five stools sat with a handheld microphone on each. The first senior announced by Principal Harrison was Rex Bradley, the senior class valedictorian and a popular member of the baseball team. No surprise there. Next was the captain of the football team, Trevor Singletary. No surprise either. Trevor was well-liked and played several sports. Trevor was followed by the head cheerleader, Veronica Phillips—Ronni as she liked to be called. She was popular and had a fun personality. She drew a large round of applause as she smiled and took her place. She was followed by the senior class president and Lucas' close friend, Cody Peterson, who was quite well-liked by members of all classes, not just the senior class.

It was already an impressive group. And with one senior remaining to be named, the crowd seemed to lean forward in anticipation.

Principal Harrison paused for a few seconds before saying, "And the fifth senior you voted to hear from today is Lucas Matthews."

When Lucas walked out from behind the curtain, the auditorium erupted in claps and loud cheers. Lucas hesitated, surprised at the reception. He could feel himself blushing.

Jill and Meg exchanged proud looks as they clapped and cheered with everyone else when Lucas walked onto the stage. He'd complained about them taking him shopping for something to wear today, but he looked like a million bucks in his dark gray dress pants, navy blazer, and the collarless white knit shirt Jill had picked out for him and insisted he wear. His mop of golden-brown hair shone under the spotlights. Surprised, Lucas half waved to the crowd before walking over to take his seat beside the other four seniors.

Jill couldn't help but be amazed and impressed by Lucas as she watched him pick up his microphone and sit down, grinning embarrassedly at the other four on stage. He was so quiet and unassuming. He always did his best to turn attention away from himself, but today, he was getting a lot of attention and recognition, and she thought he deserved every bit of it.

Lucas hadn't heard the talk that continued to circulate about him around school, but Jill had heard it. She'd heard people talking about how they respected and admired Lucas, not just for his bravery last fall, but for how genuinely nice he was to everyone. He'd grown up in the worst circumstances, but he'd come out on top. He was smart, strong, confident, kind, thoughtful, generous, and handsome. The list could go on. She was crazy about him and had been since first grade.

The principal finally quietened the room as the five seniors turned toward him, waiting for the first question.

Lucas nervously looked out across the packed auditorium. Students filled every seat while teachers and faculty stood along the sides and at the back. Coach happened to stand below one of the canned ceiling lights underneath the balcony, so Lucas was able to pick him out easily. As Principal Harrison went on and explained the question-and-answer format of the program, Lucas looked for Jill and Meg but with the bright lights on the stage and the auditorium dark, he couldn't see them.

Lucas' attention was brought back to Principal Harrison when he quipped, "Now, seniors, for our first question, we'll start with something simple like...who's your favorite principal?"

Lucas grinned along with the others as the crowd laughed and booed. The principal laughed along with them. "Okay, okay...Here's the real first question: "What was your favorite course at Fort Collins High and how will it help you in your career?"

The answers varied, and Principal Harrison had a quip to make about each answer. Some answers were funny while others were thoughtful. Trevor Singletary, captain of the football team, said his favorite subject was football. Principal Harrison rolled his eyes and shook his head, making everyone laugh.

When it came Lucas' turn, Principal Harrison said, "Well, Lucas what was your favorite course and how do you think it will help you in your career?"

The trial's intense cross examination flashed through Lucas' mind, causing him to hesitate. He cleared his throat nervously before finally holding the microphone up to answer.

"I would have to say science and chemistry are my favorite subjects if I can say two. And the reason they're my favorites is because science plays an important role in well ... everything and provides insight into every aspect of life. Chemistry is important because of the way chemicals interact with each other from the simplest to the most complex. And it affects everyday life too because everything is a combination of things. I guess it's easiest to sum it up and just say because science and chemistry are basic to everything."

Principal Harrison nodded thoughtfully. "That's an excellent answer. I guess I'd never thought of it quite that way before. I usually just have to deal with squealing girls when it's time to dissect frogs. Oh wait, that's biology!"

Everyone laughed, and Lucas relaxed. This wasn't going to be so bad after all.

"Okay, as a follow up to that question: who has been your favorite teacher and why?"

Once again, the answers varied with sometimes interesting and sometimes funny answers.

"Well, I guess if I want to eat when I go home tonight, my answer would have to be Coach Holmes," Lucas said when his turn came.

Everyone laughed and Coach Holmes waved him off from the back of the auditorium.

Lucas chuckled. "But in all seriousness, my answer to that question would still be Coach Holmes. He gives his all to his students, whether in the classroom discussing

American history or on the football field or at home around the dinner table. He's always the same, good man. It's been an incredible opportunity to be a student of his and to have the opportunity to be on his football team. Oh, and he grills a pretty mean burger too."

Lucas gave a mock salute to Coach Holmes who looked embarrassed but pleased as the crowd gave an enthusiastic round of applause.

"Alright, seniors we have just a couple more questions for you," Principal Harrison went on. "Next one: name a memory that really stands out for you or made a significant impact on your life. It doesn't have to be school-related. Just something special to you."

The auditorium grew especially still when it was Lucas' turn to answer. After hearing the question, it seemed everyone assumed Lucas would talk about what happened in the field house locker room last fall.

But Lucas had known right off what he'd say. It was simple really.

Lucas turned and looked toward the back of the auditorium where Coach had just been joined by Patsy. "The memory that stands out for me and has impacted my life the most was the minute I walked into Coach and Patsy's house for the first time. After being bounced from one foster home to another and not having a home, a real home or anyone who truly cared about me for so long, I knew in that very minute I was *finally*, really and truly home. It's a moment I'll never—ever—forget."

The auditorium went completely silent. Lucas put his hand over his heart and then held it out to Coach and Patsy who were both in the back, smiling and wiping at sudden happy tears.

Lucas then added, "Oh yeah, and I got stuck with a little sister in the deal too," breaking the spell that had gripped the auditorium as everyone laughed and applauded.

Meg mockingly shook a fist at Lucas but beamed a huge smile up at him.

Principal Harrison cleared his throat. "Okay, last question seniors. Where are you going to college, what's your major, and what do you plan to do with it?"

As each of the four ahead of him gave their answers, Lucas was impressed. He already knew some of their plans but also found out some had scholarships to big name schools while others had already started an associate's program at the local junior college to get ahead at a four-year college. Even Cody Peterson had an impressive college lined up and a couple of scholarships.

Principal Harrison asked the question again before Lucas answered.

"And Lucas. How about you? What are your plans?"

Lucas held the microphone up. "Wow. I'm impressed with everyone's plans and the scholarships they've received. Truly. That's all so awesome. It's an honor to be up here with you. As for me, I'm going into the fire service. I plan to be a firefighter and a paramedic."

"And why did you choose that profession, Lucas?" Principal Harrison asked. He knew the answer but wanted everyone else to hear it.

"Well, sir, it gives me the most opportunity to help people. And that's what I want to do with my life— help people."

Principal Harrison smiled, pleased, as he looked at the crowd, who seemed to be simultaneously fascinated and impressed by Lucas. They couldn't seem to get enough of him and his answers. Principal Harrison had heard the talk about Lucas around campus too and as it turns out, it was all actually true. While unassuming and quiet, Lucas was indeed a *very* impressive young man.

L UCAS HAD DONE INCREDIBLY well, Jill thought. He seemed so comfortable on stage and the answers he'd given had been the perfect balance of funny, sincere, and thoughtful. But as her dad walked onto the stage, Jill sat up in her seat. She knew this moment was coming. Lucas did not.

Lucas saw Jill's dad, Lt. Colonel Daniel Barkley, walk onto the stage and shake hands with Principal Harrison before moving to the podium. He was in his dress uniform and looked very serious, much more serious than he did at the dinner table where Lucas often joined their family. The auditorium quietened. This was something new for Senior Sound Off.

"Students, my name is Lt. Colonel Daniel Barkley. I am assistant base commander here at the Fort Collins Army base. We moved here in the fall, and I believe most of you know my daughter, Jill. What you may or may not know is that our family met Lucas Matthews when he and Jill were in first grade together. Not too far into the school year, Lucas' dad, Lt. Jonathan Matthews, was killed in a base training accident, and Lucas and his mother soon moved away with no way to find them at the time. When Jill saw Lucas here, she was overjoyed to see him again, as were her mother and I. When Jill told me about the Senior Sound Off program this school does, I asked Principal Harrison if I might use this opportunity to make a presentation which has been waiting for twelve years to be made. Lucas, would you please join me at the podium?"

Caught by surprise, Lucas stiffened. He stood and walked hesitantly to stand by Lt. Colonel Barkley, who looked Lucas in the eye for several seconds. Putting a hand on Lucas' shoulder, Lt. Colonel Barkley turned back to the microphone and began, "Lt. Jonathan Matthews, Lucas' dad, was killed in an Army training accident on October 9, 2000."

Lucas flushed and looked down, feeling himself grow hot.

Lt Colonel Barkley continued. "Lt. Matthews was piloting a Blackhawk helicopter on a training exercise when the engine malfunctioned. The helicopter crashed, killing one solider on impact and seriously wounding the other three, including Lt. Matthews. Lt. Matthews managed to get the two wounded soldiers to safety while being seriously wounded himself. While in the process of retrieving the remains of the solder killed, the helicopter's fuel line exploded, killing Lt. Matthews instantly. While losing his life, he saved two others. At the time, the Army granted the Soldier's Medal to Lt. Matthews posthumously, the highest peacetime award for an act of heroism in a noncombatant situation. On behalf of a grateful nation, I would like to present this medal to you, Lucas Matthews, Lt. Matthews' son, with our thanks and admiration for the exemplary soldier your dad was in serving not only his country but his fellow soldiers. It looks like Jon's son takes after his father."

Lt. Colonel Barkley smiled a proud smile at Lucas whose eyes had widened as he opened the case holding a beautiful silver medal and handed it reverently to Lucas.

"Very few of these medals are ever awarded, Lucas. This is very special, and I believe you, more than anyone I've ever known, deserve it on your dad's behalf. It was a privilege to know and serve with your dad, and I know he would be so incredibly proud of you today. Congratulations."

Lucas looked from the medal back to Lt. Colonel Barkley and back to the medal, never hearing the thunderous applause that had erupted. He knew his dad had been killed in a training accident, but he'd never been told the circumstances and never knew he'd also saved lives. Lt.

Colonel Barkley stuck his hand out and took Lucas' hand, shaking it firmly. The sound of applause and cheering gradually registered on Lucas, and he looked out at the packed auditorium as if surprised to see people there.

While the applause continued, Lucas managed to say to Lt. Colonel Barkley, his mouth suddenly dry, "Thank you, sir. I never knew..."

"I know, Lucas. I know. We thought it was high time you did. Your dad was a great friend, a great officer, and a great soldier. I'm proud to have known him and to know you."

Lt. Colonel Barkley patted Lucas' shoulder and turned to leave. Lucas walked slowly back to his stool, never taking his eyes off the medal in his hands. Lost in his thoughts, Lucas didn't know Principal Harrison had dismissed the assembly until Cody Peterson on the stool next to him gave him a good-natured shove, and Lucas saw the auditorium emptying.

CODY PEERED OVER LUCAS' shoulder to see the medal as did the other seniors on the stage. They gathered around Lucas, taking a turn to either shake his hand or give him a quick hug of congratulations. Lucas could see Coach and Patsy, making their way to the stage. Not too far behind them were Jill and Meg.

He quickly acknowledged all of those around him then made his way down the small set of stairs on the side of the stage to meet Jill and his family. Patsy grabbed Lucas into a tight hug and didn't let go until Coach cleared his throat and Patsy stepped away, dabbing her eyes.

"So proud of you, Son," Coach said before he gave him a firm embrace "You couldn't have made either of us prouder." He put his arm around Patsy and pulled her into the hug.

"I meant every word," Lucas said, looking between the two of them with a smile, love on his face.

"Even what you said about getting stuck with a little sister?!" Meg teased as she grabbed his arm. She turned him around to face her and hugged him tightly.

Everyone laughed.

"Oh, I especially meant that," Lucas said, laughing as he gave her a hug.

Jill came up beside him and shyly took his hand. Lucas pulled her close beside him and squeezed her hand in response.

"I'm so, so proud of you, Lucas," Jill said, beaming up at him.

Lucas blushed as Jill gave him a quick peck on the cheek, exchanging a lingering look that meant a whole lot more.

L UCAS NEVER REALIZED HOW much fun the last week of school was going to be as a senior. There were the boring rehearsals for commencement and baccalaureate, of course, but then there had been other parties and celebrations throughout the week. Receiving his dad's medal and Senior Sound Off had, so far, been the highlights of the week. Lucas had carefully placed the case with its medal on his nightstand. He wanted the medal to be the first thing he saw in the morning and the last thing he'd see when he went to bed at night—a daily reminder to honor his dad's legacy.

The formal ceremonies and assemblies were over, with the exception of commencement tomorrow night. But tonight was family night. Coach and Patsy invited Jill and her parents over for dinner for the chance to relax and visit. Coach grilled steaks and Patsy and Jill's mom pulled out all of the stops for the rest of the meal. It was a veritable feast.

They ate on the patio and enjoyed the pleasant spring evening. Lucas tried to stop them, but the Barkley's insisted on telling stories about Lucas as a first-grader and some of the mischief he and Jill had gotten into together.

Lucas blushed when Meg reached over and laughingly pinched his cheek. "I bet he was just the cutest little fella!"

Jill smiled and said, "And he still is!" causing Lucas to blush again.

Dan Barkley talked about Lucas' dad—what he'd been like, some funny stories about his antics at boot camp, and his excitement at becoming commanding officer on a Blackhawk helicopter. Dan and Jessica talked about what good friends Lucas' parents had been to them and how much fun their families had had together. Jessica commented on how much Lucas looked like his dad and how Lucas even had some of his dad's mannerisms. Lucas listened raptly. Getting to hear about his mom and dad from friends who had known them so well made Lucas feel closer to his parents than he ever had before.

After dinner, Dan Barkley mysteriously disappeared into the house and reappeared minutes later carrying an official-looking envelope. He settled back into his chair and took a long drink of sweet tea before straightening and turning to Lucas.

"Lucas, graduating from high school is a major step in life. But it's just one step. You've already been through a lot in your short life and coped with it far better than many adults ever could. With your parents being such good friends of ours, we want to do what we can to help give you a good start. We know your mom and dad would want that for you too.

"Upon your dad's death, the designated amount of funds for soldiers who die in the line of duty went into an account for you and your mother. With your mother's leaving so abruptly, we didn't have the chance to tell her about the money. And even though we searched by every means possible, we couldn't find the two of you. This has been sitting in an account, waiting for you, all these years."

He handed Lucas the envelope.

"That envelope contains information about those funds and the account that had been set up. You will be able to pull the amount you need to pay for educational purposes, such as the firefighters' academy and the paramedic training program. Plus, there will be a nice-size amount left over. That balance will continue to be held in trust until you reach twenty-one and then, the full amount will be available to you and yours to do with as you wish."

Dan slid a glance at Jill, who was smiling at Lucas excitedly.

Lucas was speechless. He took the envelope from Dan and held it in his hand, staring at it. His dad had made sure, in a way, to take care of Lucas and his future. The money was here, in his hand, when he needed it most. He was going to the firefighting academy and paramedic training without having to worry about paying for either of them. The relief was enormous, and Lucas could only look around the table with what he was sure must be a dumbstruck look.

"Wow...I..." Lucas began just as Coach's cell phone rang and excited talk erupted around the table.

Glancing at his phone, Coach stood and stepped inside the house to take the call. Coming back a couple of minutes later, a somber look on his face, he resumed his seat and took Patsy's hand. The talk died down as everyone looked at him expectantly.

"What is it, Craig?" Patsy asked anxiously.

Coach took a deep breath and looked at Lucas.

"That was Thomas Bender."

Lucas' breath hitched. He'd heard the trial was winding down.

"And?" Lucas asked, taking Jill's hand and squeezing it.

"It only took the jury ten minutes to find all three boys guilty on every charge. Sentencing will be next week. He asked me to thank you again for your testimony. When they polled the jury members, many said that was what clenched the guilty verdict from them. You did well, Son."

Lucas looked around the table with a reluctant smile.

"And Lucas, there's one more thing," Coach added with a hesitant look at Patsy. "He asked if you wanted to make a victim's statement at the sentencing."

Silence hung in the air as Lucas looked from Coach to the anxious faces around the table watching him.

"Is that something I *have* to do?" Lucas asked softly.

"No, you don't if you'd rather not. But..." Coach paused, weighing what he said next.

"But what, sir?" Lucas asked.

Coach took a deep breath. "What they did... What they did..." Coach paused, a catch in his voice. "Lucas, I'm just so sorry I didn't recognize what was going on. I could have put a stop to it but I was too..."

"Coach, no. Stop. I could have told you at any time," Lucas hurriedly interjected. "It was just my battle to fight. You have nothing to feel bad about. Really." Lucas looked at Coach, his eyes pleading for Coach's understanding.

Coach cleared his throat and went on. "Lucas, you're a strong young man. You continue to amaze me. The choice of whether to make a statement or not is totally up to you. It's not an easy decision. But just know, and I think I can speak for everyone here, we will support you no matter what you decide."

Nodding, Dan Barkley agreed. "Yes, Lucas—it's up to you. You're the one that's been impacted the most by their actions. Your statement will only speak to how the actions *they* chose to take against you have affected you. And only you can speak to that. The power of your statement could make the difference between a more lenient or lengthy sentence. But remember, it was *their* choice and *their* actions—not yours—that put them in the situation they're in. You're only saying how you've been affected."

Lucas nodded silently. He looked down, still holding Jill's hand tightly.

"Lucas?" Meg said softly.

Lucas looked up expectantly.

Meg smiled shyly and said, "They're all three despicable, and I hope to never see any of them again. But we also have something we should all be very grateful to them for."

Realizing what Meg meant, Lucas began to smile.

"And just what could we possibly have to thank those three for?" Patsy asked with a huff.

"We have Lucas," Meg said softly, taking hold of Lucas' other hand and looking up at him with a smile. "Lucas stepping in between me and those bullies in middle school? That's what brought him to us. And for that, I'll forever be thankful to them."

Silence hung in the air as Meg looked at Lucas, love and admiration in her eyes. She looked away after several breathless seconds and squeezed Lucas' hand before quipping, "Well, okay then . . .what's for dessert?" making everyone laugh.

After the laughter died down, Lucas somberly looked around the table. "I . . . I just don't know what to say. This is all a lot to process. I'm just glad the trial is in the past. I'll think about giving a statement, but tonight, I just want to think about graduating and the future. And I promise, I'll put this to good use," he said, holding up the envelope.

"We have no doubt," Dan said, chuckling as Jessica nodded and grinned her agreement.

Patsy and Jessica exchanged smiles and began clearing the dinner dishes to serve dessert.

"In fact, I won't be surprised if you're not promoted to chief within a year," Dan said as Patsy set a plate with a huge piece of chocolate cake and ice cream in front him.

Everyone laughed, Lucas laughing along with them. He'd been thinking about his career in the fire service for a long time. He was going to work hard, study hard, and do whatever he could to learn everything there was to learn and advance through the ranks. Mr. Andy and Mrs. Garrett had ignited this dream in him. As a big part of that dream, he wanted to go back to Abernathy as an officer, maybe even a chief, and make them proud. Lucas smiled as he looked around the table.

Yeah. He had a plan.

Lucas could hear grumbling coming from Coach's office. He laid his mortar board with its gold tassel on the back of the sofa and with a soft knock on the door, walked into Coach's office. Coach was focused on a tiny mirror tucked into a back corner, working feverishly with a necktie.

"What's going on, Coach?" Lucas asked with a grin. "That necktie getting the better of you?"

Coach turned, sending a teasing snarl Lucas' direction.

"Just about the time I think I've got it, something goes wrong. But I think I'm just...about...there."

Coach pulled the final length of the tie through and adjusted the knot at his neck, giving it one final tug.

"I tell you one thing; I sure am glad I don't have to wear one of these things every day. What a pain!"

Lucas chuckled. "Couldn't agree with you more."

Looking in the mirror, Coach gave the tie one final appraisal before stepping back to his desk. "Well, looks like you got your tie done with no problem," he commented, glancing down at the tie showing at the neck of Lucas' graduation gown.

"I've had lots of practice lately," Lucas said with a slight eye roll.

Coach stopped and nodded solemnly. "Unfortunately, yes you have. But what about today—you ready? You look quite distinguished in your robe. Well actually," Coach said studying him then breaking into a grin, "you kinda look like a crow."

Lucas chuckled but then Coach said in a serious tone, "High school graduation is a big thing, you know."

"Oh I know. And I'm ready," Lucas said, his laughter gradually dying away. "Everything has . . . well, everything's been kinda nice leading up to today. I never knew being a senior would be so much fun. And sir, I know I wouldn't have been able to have the fun I've had or enjoyed this year or the last four years of school if it hadn't been for you, Patsy, Meg . . ." Lucas trailed off, reaching over and aimlessly shuffling some loose paper clips on Coach's desk.

"Something on your mind, Lucas?" Coach asked, sensing Lucas was leading up to something in his quiet way.

Lucas looked up and pushing the paper clips away, he sat down heavily in the nearest guest chair.

"Yes, sir. Actually, there is," Lucas said and then paused so long Coach wondered if he was going to continue.

"It's about the sentencing hearing coming up," Lucas finally said softly. "Mr. Bender emailed and said it's Tuesday afternoon. And he said again he'd like for me to be there and say something."

Coach nodded once and waited for Lucas to continue.

"Coach, I've done a lot of thinking about it and…and…I think I need to do it." He paused and looked up at Coach who was studying him thoughtfully. "But what do you think?"

"Lucas, I trust your judgment. If you feel it's important that you say something, I'd say do it. I have to admit, I am glad you're thinking in that direction. Those boys are young and had their whole lives ahead of them but after what they've done, most especially to you over the years, as your father, I hope they lock them up and throw away the key. But, please, don't say that in your statement!" he added with a chuckle.

Lucas gave a light laugh that ended in a sigh.

"Yes, sir," Lucas said with a nod before standing. "Thank you for your time. And speaking of time," Lucas said pulling his phone from under his robe and tapping the screen. "I've got to get to school. Nate said he'd wait for me before we line up.

"I think Patsy and Meg are about ready," Coach said, standing and holding his crossed fingers in the air. "We'll see you there."

Lucas grinned and headed toward the door.

"And Lucas," Coach called after him, "we'll be the ones cheering the loudest when you walk across that stage."

THREE DAYS LATER, LUCAS sat in the same courtroom where he'd testified just a few weeks earlier. This time he sat in a seat next to Meg with Coach and Patsy on the other side of her. Their seats were in a special section directly behind Mr. Bender, reserved for those slated to speak. Officer Jenkins, along with Jill and her parents, sat a few rows back. There was a low hum of conversation in the room as everyone waited for the defendants to be brought in and the judge to arrive. Lucas hunched over, rubbing the palms of his hands across his thighs and cleared his throat nervously several times.

"This is going to be easy," Meg leaned over and said into Lucas' ear. "You just have to read what you wrote. You don't even have to look at them if you don't want to."

Lucas nodded, knowing it really wasn't going to be that easy. He felt emotions churning inside that he had fought for years to suppress. He had his statement prepared but he felt himself uncharacteristically teetering on the edge of maintaining that rigid control and not being able to hold it in any longer. He was resigned to making the statement, knowing it was something he needed to do, but just wasn't sure what might happen in the process.

Lucas sat up when the side door opened and Joel, Marty, and Tony filed out behind one of the court police officers and were directed to the same tables where they'd sat during the trial, their attorneys already in place. The three walked in, heads down, not looking at anyone in the room even though Lucas had noticed the parents of each were seated in a similar area behind them as where he and the Holmes sat.

The bailiff announced the judge and after everyone stood and sat back down, the proceedings started immediately.

"Mr. Jacobs, you may make your statement please."

The defense attorney rose and spoke briefly about the young ages of the defendants, how they could still lead a good, productive life after prison if they received a more lenient sentence, and how distraught their families were at the situation.

The judge then invited members of the three's families to speak. Each set of parents spoke, telling what a good boy their son actually was, that he'd fallen in with the wrong crowd, he didn't realize the severity of his actions and on and on, imploring the judge's lenient decision with a lot of tears.

When Marty Pierce's parents had spoken, the last of the three couples, the judge turned to Mr. Bender, and Lucas took a deep breath and let it out slowly.

"Mr. Bender, your statement please."

Lucas' heart began to pound as Mr. Bender made a few remarks about the three defendants being found guilty by a jury of their peers and how the consequences of their actions should correlate with what might have been deadly and far-reaching implications if they hadn't been stopped and caught.

"I can only speak to the perceived implications of their actions," Mr. Bender said. "But the primary victim of their actions—from cruelty and harassment to drug dealing, and yes, even attempted murder can speak firsthand about how their actions have affected his life. I invite Lucas Matthews to the podium to speak, Your Honor."

Lucas took one more fortifying breath as the judge nodded and motioned for Lucas to come forward. Mr. Bender gave Lucas a curt nod and pat on the shoulder as they passed in the aisle.

As Lucas removed the paper containing his statement from his pocket, he could see from the corner of his eye that the three had finally looked up and turned their heads toward him. He wasn't sure if this was one final act of defiance or an attempt at intimidation, but it wasn't going to work.

Lucas spread his paper slowly and methodically onto the podium as he cleared his throat. He purposefully turned and looked Joel, Marty, and Tony each in the eye for several long seconds before turning back to face the judge.

"If it pleases the court," Lucas began in a steady voice, "thank you for this opportunity to speak as to how the actions of Joel De Grey, Marty Pierce, and Tony Harlow have affected me personally. From our first encounter in middle school when the three jumped me in a three to one fight, through the next four years of bullying, and up until they tried to force me into a drug overdose, these three have continually sought through various methods to harass and intimidate me.

"It has been an ongoing and painful experience, both emotionally and physically. But then my sister, Meg, wisely reminded me of something just a few nights ago that made me think of this in a completely different light."

Lucas paused and sniffed, running his hand quickly beneath his nose before continuing.

"Your Honor, since both of my parents died, I have been in foster care the majority of my life. I've bounced from house to house and family to family, most of them not caring one bit about me. I realized that early on, and came to believe, that I was alone in this world and only had myself to depend on. When these three drug me into that alley in middle school, I just thought it was more of the same of what I'd experienced for years and expected the same outcome.

"But then … but then …" Lucas stopped, looking down and gripping the podium until his knuckles turned white. He was unable to go on for several long seconds. The silence in the courtroom was deafening.

Meg stood quietly and walked to Lucas' side and placed her hand on his arm. Lucas glanced at her, sniffing, and swiping at a tear before taking her hand and holding it tightly.

"But then," he started again, his voice a bit firmer, "that incident brought me into contact with Coach, Patsy, and Meg Holmes. They brought me into their home. And the past four years have been the happiest of my life. I have a family—maybe not a biological family—but a loving, caring family who have welcomed me and treated me like I'd always been one of theirs and considered me a son. In a way, I have them to thank for that," Lucas said, looking at Joel, Marty, and Tony, their eyes round as they listened.

Lucas paused again, still clutching the podium and Meg's hand tightly.

"That night in the locker room when they forced that drug down my throat, I knew I was going to die, and I wasn't afraid. But what I was afraid of . . ."

Suddenly, after years of forcing tears away, of pressing down the pain, of trying to ignore the rejections, the insults, the insecurities, and the uncertainties he'd navigated most of his life— everything came crashing together in that moment. Lucas had to stop again, unable to stem the onslaught of tears that suddenly overwhelmed him. His shoulders shook with the intensity of the emotions engulfing him.

Glancing at each other, Coach and Patsy stood and walked to stand beside Lucas. Patsy stood on Lucas' other side, her hands on his arm, while Coach placed a reassuring hand on Lucas' shoulder.

Lucas cleared his throat forcefully and finally managed to say, "I wasn't afraid to die. But I . . . I didn't want to be the cause of any pain, or to remind the Holmes of their son, Avery, who died from a drug incident not long before I came to live with them. The Holmes have been good to me, very good. I just didn't want to be the cause of any more suffering for them."

Lucas stopped and ran his hand down his face, wiping away some of the tears. He cleared his throat and looking at the judge said, "I'm thankful to Officer Jenkins, who saved my life that afternoon, but I'll always be thankful to the

Holmes for loving me and saving my life in every other way. Thank you, sir."

Lucas turned to Patsy, who enveloped him in a tight embrace as his body was wracked with sobs. Lucas reached out to put an arm around Meg, pulling her close while Coach put his arms around the three of them and held them all close, all four oblivious to the onlookers where there wasn't a dry eye to be found.

Lucas held the three of them close before giving them a watery but bright smile, filled with love and relief. They moved apart and then stepped back to their seats. The judge took a breath and turned to look at the defendants.

"Will the defendants please rise?" he asked in a raspy voice.

Joel, Marty, and Tony, along with each of their attorneys, reluctantly stood and faced the judge.

"Gentlemen, you have been fairly tried in a court of law and found guilty by a jury of your peers of a wide array of charges up to and including drug dealing and attempted murder. From everything that has been presented both during the trial and today, it is evident the three of you have a lengthy track record of abusive behavior that has progressed to the point of attempted murder. And this attempt would have been completed without the timely arrival of law enforcement.

"I detect no remorse and have serious concerns as to whether any one of you have the ability or, more importantly, the desire to change. The length of the sentence to be imposed is entirely at my discretion within certain limits prescribed by the law. After the compelling statement given today, it is my ruling to sentence each of you to the maximum afforded in cases such as this. You are therefore sentenced to life in prison with the possibility of parole, with good behavior, in seventy-five years."

The mouths of the three dropped open as their attorneys erupted into protest. Their parents gasped and began to protest loudly as well.

"Order in this court," the judge said forcefully as he banged his gavel several times. "I will hold anyone who does not sit down and keep their mouth shut in contempt of this court, which includes jail time. I strongly encourage everyone to come to order."

He banged his gavel one more time before the bailiff asked everyone to rise as the judge left through the door behind his desk. Dazed, the three convicted defendants, their shoulders slumped, were handcuffed and ushered quickly from the courtroom.

Lucas sat motionless, spent. He leaned over, putting his head in his hands while those around him stood and began talking. He felt the pats on the back and heard snatches of things being said, but he knew instinctively the minute Jill placed a hand on his shoulder.

"I am so incredibly proud of you," Jill whispered softly in his ear.

Lucas grabbed her hand, holding it tightly as he stood and smiled at her, his eyes shining with relief and happiness.

"Lucas," Coach said, pride and love on his face as he squeezed Lucas' shoulder, "come on, Son. Let's go home."

Lucas smiled.

Home.

TEN MONTHS LATER…

T HE TWENTY-FOUR NEWLY GRADUATED firefighter recruits stood in a row across the stage in the auditorium at District Five's headquarters. The District Five Chief, along with several city chiefs from across the district, filled the seats behind the podium, their badges and brass bugle lapel pins shining under the stage's bright lights. The speeches had just concluded, and the moment had arrived when the new recruits would take the oath of office and have their badge pinned on.

Today culminated nine months of marked study, drills, and training. Paramedic training had been intense but fascinating, and Lucas had breezed through it, leaning on his love of science and chemistry from high school. The firefighting section had been everything he'd dreamed of—even better than how Mr. Andy had described it. It had been thrilling, tough, daunting, and the most exciting thing Lucas had ever done. He'd loved every second. The physical training was grueling but after football drills in the Texas heat in August, it actually hadn't been too bad. Whatever ache, pain, or discomfort he'd felt at the time, it was all worth it. He may be a lowly rookie right now, but that was just temporary. He was going to work hard and make sure that changed as quickly as possible.

From the glare of the spotlights on the stage, Lucas strained to look into the darkened auditorium and the sea of faces in the audience, proud families and friends who had come to watch. Lucas finally found Coach and Patsy and then Meg's eager face, craning to find him on stage. When she saw him, she gave a big wave. He bit back a smile. Dan and Jessica Barkley sat beside them. And Jill. He looked down to the front row where Jill sat, beaming up at him, excitement and happiness in her blue eyes.

FROM HER FRONT ROW seat, Jill watched as Lucas and the other academy graduates stood, raised their right hand and took their oath of office. Lucas' face almost seemed to glow with happiness. He'd been working his entire life toward this moment and had endured and overcome a lot to get there. He'd become successful even beyond what he'd admitted to her were his wildest dreams. He was kind and good, but he was also strong and determined. She wanted the world for him because she loved him. She loved him with her whole heart.

She glanced down and wiggled the fingers on her left hand as the bright lights from the stage caught the diamonds in the engagement ring Lucas had given her last weekend. In his quiet, unassuming way, he'd asked her dad for his permission and that same evening had dropped to one knee in front of her as they'd walked in the dusk of a chilly spring evening alongside a small pond in their favorite park. His sweet, earnest proposal left her in tears as she took out her trembling left hand and Lucas slid the most amazing engagement ring she'd ever seen onto her finger. They'd kissed as if they'd never kissed before. From that moment on, Jill felt as if she were in a dream—one she never wanted to wake from.

Those on either side of her stood, bringing Jill back to the present as the oath was administered. The District Five Chief asked those pinning a badge on their firefighter to step up and stand directly in front of them. As Jill stepped up and stood in front of Lucas, he grinned into her upturned face. She looked nervous. No, she *was* nervous, he realized. They'd practiced the pinning several times so she would feel comfortable when it came time, but her hands were trembling as she held Lucas' badge up to the left side of his uniform shirt, waiting for the word from the chief.

Lucas looked down, seeing the engagement ring sparkling on Jill's trembling left hand.

"I love you," Lucas whispered softly so only Jill could hear.

Her hands stilled as she smiled bashfully up at him with a look filled with love.

"I love you more," she whispered back, causing Lucas to grin.

When the signal came, Jill pinned Lucas' badge to his uniform perfectly and then placed her hands softly on his chest before she, along with the others, took a step back and exchanged a proud smile between them.

Lucas sneaked a quick look at the badge he'd dreamed of, the badge he had worked so hard to have, resting firmly over his heart. He smiled to himself as Mr. Andy's words came back to him: *A badge shines brighter because of the hard work and sacrifice it took to achieve.* How true, Lucas thought, how very true.

"Congratulations, Rookies!" the chief said from the podium. "Before each of you go to your new department and take up residence in the station you're assigned, let me leave you with this. Always, always put safety first out there. Look at who is standing in front of you. And remember, behind every first responder is a loved one waiting for you to come home. You are now dismissed. It's been a pleasure having you at the District Fire Academy. But now, it's time to celebrate your accomplishments with your friends and family."

Lucas took Jill's hand as they turned to step from the stage together into the future—their future—that looked brighter than ever. The possibilities were limitless.

# ACKNOWLEDGMENTS

RECOGNIZING ALL OF THOSE who have contributed to this book is a daunting task. There are so many who have encouraged me and let me know they are anxiously waiting this installment of the Beyond the Badge Series. But this first foray into writing a young adult novel would never have happened, or even been conceived, if not for Sandy Saucier. After being my beta reader for *Brothers in Service,* Sandy asked what I planned to write next. I told her the third novel in the series, picking up where *Brotherhood By Fire* leaves off with Lucas and incorporating characters from both books. Sandy said, "You should write a young adult novel about Lucas and the intervening years." As soon as Sandy said that light bulbs started flashing. Yes! It was a BRILLIANT idea and thus, *To Become A Brother* had its beginning. Sandy never ceases to support, encourage, share her brilliant ideas, and is an amazing sounding board. Thank you, Sandy! This book wouldn't be here if it hadn't been for your very timely and insightful suggestion.

And my two beta readers who I unabashedly must say are the most awesomest and bestest beta readers ever!

Bennett and Emma Bell, my great nephew and great niece. They took time to read the first draft of each chapter, answered my questions, made suggestions, shared ideas, gave me thumbs up and thumbs down where needed, plus shared their excitement and enthusiastic support all along the way. And I would be remiss not to mention my great niece, Bree Bell, too. While Bennett and Emma were reading the book, Bree was sending me messages with her love, support, and big smile. What an inspiration these three are to me! Thank you, Bennett, Emma, and Bree!

To Brandon Pollock, voice actor for the Beyond the Badge series and dear friend—thank you! You have been such a cheerleader, encourager, and supporter all along the way and that means more than I can ever say. While you are a true professional, you're an even better friend. I appreciate you and enjoy the process and opportunity of working with you.

Sean Linton has once again done a masterful job of editing and raised the bar in *To Become A Brother*. The things Sean catches absolutely amaze me and make the book stronger and better every step of the way.

Many, many thanks to Dayna Linton of the Day Agency whose professionalism help, friendship, encouragement, and unwavering support in bringing my books to paperback and ebook are appreciated beyond what words can say. Thank you, Dayna—You. Are. Awesome!

To the many, many friends who have been so incredibly supportive - wow! You make writing even more fun and rewarding with your excitement, encouragement, and anxiousness to read 'my next.' Thank you for your support and love. It absolutely means the world to me.

A very special thank you to my sweet Mom who listens patiently as I rattle on about my books, and my plans, and my ideas, and . . . on and on into infinity as I'm sure she feels at times. Her support and faith in my writing never waivers and it's what I lean on most when I'm having a difficult day. From the bottom of my heart, I love you and thank you, Mom!

I have an awesome family and appreciate the support and encouragement they've given from helping with advice and technical issues in the books, to selling books, to coming to author events and supporting me in person. Words are just inadequate to convey how much that means to me. Thank you, Larry and Danette, and Zac and Liz! I love you all SO much!

I owe the biggest thank you of all to the Lord who gave me what so many have said is the gift of writing. Many times when I go back and read parts of the books, I think - did I really write that? That makes me smile because that's when I know the Lord is sharing through me. When I look back on how some things have come together both in the books and in life, it can only be attributed to God's steady and all-knowing hand. And as always, anything that resonates with you as a reader, is a result of the gift that God has graciously seen fit to share through me.

# ABOUT THE AUTHOR

LINDY BELL IS AN avid reader and has been her entire life, enjoying a wide variety of genres. Lindy's love of reading led to her love of writing. *To Become A Brother* is the young adult novel in the Beyond the Badge series and Lindy's first young adult novel to write. The first two novels in the series, *Brotherhood By Fire* and *Brothers in Service - Through Thick & Thin* have both been met with widespread acclaim by readers and firefighters alike. Both books are recognized for the intensity of the emotions they elicit as well as the powerfully accurate portrayals of the fire service. Her first book, *Jane Austen Celebrates, Holidays & Occasions Regency Style*, tracks each month's holidays and how they have evolved and been celebrated through the centuries.

Lindy's writing has also brought about opportunities to speak to a variety of groups as well as teach Adult Professional Education courses on Jane Austen and the Regency Era at Southern Methodist University (SMU). Lindy also presents live book reviews to book clubs across the Dallas/Fort Worth Metroplex and writes book reviews for the Novels Alive blog site. Lindy is a graduate of Abilene

Christian University with a Bachelors degree in Business Administration.

When not writing, Lindy enjoys relaxing with an engaging novel, cross stitching and serving in a variety of ministries in her home congregation.

Lindy would love to hear from you! Connect with her through her website and social media links.

Website: lindybellwrites.com
X: @LindyBellWrites
Facebook.com/LindyBellWrites/
Instagram: LindyBellWrites
YouTube: @LindyBellwr